# BOOKED

## FOR THE
## *Holidays*

## ERIN HAWKINS

# AUTHOR'S NOTE

Please be advised Booked for the Holidays is a spicy romantic comedy with **open-door** romance, and **on-page** sexual content and profanity. Mature readers only.

# LAST CHRISTMAS

"I GOT IT!" I yell, careening down the stairs to rush for the front door.

I'm expecting my friend Cassie, but when I yank open the door, it's not her.

Standing on our front porch is Liam Hargrove, my brother's best friend and business partner at Jensen Innovations, the tech company they founded while they were still in college. Their cutting-edge AR/VR platform has completely transformed corporate training and made them both wildly successful (and disgustingly wealthy) in the process.

He's facing sideways, like he rang the doorbell, then turned to take in his surroundings.

It's been years since I've seen him in person, so I take advantage of the moment to ogle him. He's wearing a black mid-length wool coat with a camel-colored turtleneck underneath, dark fitted jeans, and lace-up boots. His dark hair is wild from the blustery day and he's sporting a five o'clock shadow.

The fitted denim is snug against his thighs and the way

he's gripping the neck on the wine bottle in his hand sends a thrill down my spine.

While I'm standing in the doorway, mouth agape, he turns in my direction.

"June Bug." He addresses me with an achingly handsome smile, his dark eyes alight with recognition.

At the sound of my childhood nickname, I hold in a groan. My parents can still get away with it, but I've retrained everyone in my life, including Jasper, my older brother, to stop calling me that. And there's nothing that can crush your spirit like the man of your dreams, the one you've been pining over for years, calling you by your silly childhood nickname.

He steps over the threshold and envelopes me in a hug.

The moment his strong arms wrap around me and the scent of him fills my nose, I sigh. It's woodsy and masculine, yet crisp, like the winter air around us. My body tingling in response to him is all the confirmation I need that my crush on Liam is still very much intact.

As I delight in his embrace, I let my mind wander to the past.

When Jasper and Liam were attending college together, Liam spent a few breaks and holidays with us due to the travel time and cost of returning to his parents' home in London. It was Liam's British accent that initially had me swooning. He's gorgeous and charismatic, with just enough edginess—unshaven jaw and tattoos on his arms—that screams bad boy, yet he always looks put together without even trying. Just like he does now.

It's a simple coincidence that I'm the one to answer the door for him, yet my brain is taking the opportunity to invent an entire scenario where Liam is arriving at my house as my boyfriend.

*"You're here," I say, breathless, opening the door to his beaming smile.*

*"Come here, gorgeous."*

*Then, he wraps me up in his arms and sweeps me off my feet before pressing his lips to mine.*

In reality, Liam pulls back, and I do my best to collect my swooning thoughts.

"Hey, Liam," I finally manage to squeak out. "I didn't know you were kissing—I mean, coming."

I force a smile and will myself not to blush. Please god, don't let him be able to read my thoughts.

"It was last minute." His crooked smile is the perfect mix of confidence and allure.

I motion for him to come into the foyer and take his coat. Turning away from him, I hang his coat on the rack in the corner, but before I part with it, I hold the collar up to my nose, letting the scent of him burrow itself there.

It's pathetic. It's sad. It's all I've got.

When I turn back from hanging his coat, he extends the bottle out to me.

"Happy holidays."

I read the yellow label on the bottle: Veuve Clicquot La Grande Dame Brut Rose. I'm not a champagne connoisseur, but I recognize the label and know it must be expensive.

And there goes my imagination again, pretending Liam picked out the champagne just for me.

"This is so sweet. Thank you." I beam as I cradle it in my arms like a love letter.

Liam must notice the way I'm looking at him with hearts in my eyes.

"Uh, yeah, well it's for everyone." He motions toward the house behind me.

"Right. I know."

Basking in the alone time with Liam, I stare up at him as every coherent thought in my brain refuses to make the connection with my mouth.

After an awkward pause, his brows lift. "So, is Jasper around?"

I have got to get a grip, or I'm going to embarrass myself. More than I already am.

"Uh, yeah." I motion toward our living room off the foyer. "Right this way."

As soon as Jasper and Liam spot each other, they fall into an easy, breezy, beautiful bromance. It makes me feel even sillier for being an inarticulate mess. But to be fair, I don't want a bromance with Liam, I just want him to see me as more than Jasper's little sister. And then fall desperately in love with me. Oh, and there's sex, too. Lots of toe-curling sex. That's how it would be with Liam, I imagine.

"Hey, man, why didn't you tell me you were coming?" Jasper asks, standing to greet Liam with a hug.

"Wasn't sure of my plans until this morning when I got on the plane. I hope the invitation still stands."

"Of course it stands. I'm just surprised you showed."

"You said tonight was going to be a rager, and you know I can't resist a good party."

Jasper laughs. "It's got nothing on Elton's party, but we'll try to show you a good time.

"You remember my sister, Juniper." Jasper motions to where I'm now leaning against the doorway watching them.

"Of course, I remember June Bug."

My face scrunches at the nickname. Again. *What does a girl got to do to grow up around here?*

"She's opening a bookstore soon," Jasper says.

"A romance bookstore," I add because I love Jasper, but

he doesn't know all the details of my vision. "I just signed the lease for the space last week."

Liam nods at me. "Congratulations. It must be in the Jensen blood to be an entrepreneur."

Jasper chuckles. "Yeah, but I told her I'm shit with the business side of things, and she should talk to you."

"It's fine." I throw out a dismissive wave. The visual of me rambling on about my romance bookstore dream while Liam politely nods enters my head. "I'm sure you have a million other things to do."

When my eyes find Liam's again, I swear there's something in them that wasn't there a moment ago. Like he might be looking at me differently. Like I'm a grown woman with passions and desires that intrigue him.

"Never too busy for Jas's little sis."

Or...maybe not.

*Jas's little sis?* Ugh. That's worse than June Bug.

"Let's find some time to chat tonight."

Disappointment is crushing my throat, so all I can do is nod.

At that moment, my mom walks into the living room, a gasp of excitement leaving her mouth at the sight of Liam. "Oh, Liam. You flew all the way from London for our Christmas Eve party? We're so honored."

My mom might be just as obsessed with him as I am.

"I didn't make it home to London. I was in Vancouver visiting a friend, then came here."

"Oh, well, we're very excited to have you." Mom hugs Liam. "We'll put you in the basement guest room."

"I booked a room at the Snowshoe Inn. I didn't want to impose."

"Nonsense." Mom waves him off. "You'll stay with us."

The doorbell rings.

"Oh, that must be Stella," Mom says, heading for the door with Jasper hot on her heels. His mega-watt smile somehow increases ten-fold at the mention of his girlfriend. Well, fake girlfriend, I think. He didn't confirm, but there's something suspicious about suddenly dating your childhood rival when you've been at each other's throats for nearly twenty years.

Jasper greets Stella, then we all get a turn while he looks on adoringly at her.

I wonder if that's what I look like when I smile at Liam. I wonder if my little crush is obvious to everyone else. And most of all I wonder if I'll ever experience the kind of all-consuming love that I read about in romance books.

Liam and Stella are introduced, and I feel a familiar ache—*not* jealousy, exactly, but a wishful kind of yearning. The way he teases her so easily, how she rolls her eyes like they've done this a hundred times before. I watch them, and all I can think is how I've never known how to be that effortless around him. With him, I've only ever felt like the girl with the crush, trying too hard not to show it.

While the rest of the group starts to discuss Christmas Eve party planning around me, my thoughts drift to the lease I signed this week. A perfect storefront location on Founders Street in downtown Cedar Hollow. Sandwiched between Sugar Pine Bakery and Wild Fern plant shop, it's the ideal location for my bookstore. And the space has a two-bedroom loft apartment on the upper floor for me to live in. It feels like my life is falling into place.

Now, if only I could make Liam Hargrove fall in love with me, everything would be perfect.

"Liam, do you mind going with Juniper to pick up the wine?" Mom says.

At the sound of my name, I finally tune back into the conversation around me.

"Anything to help," Liam says.

"Great!" My mom beams. "Why don't you two do that while Stella and I wrap presents and Jasper helps your dad with the decorations."

While my mom rushes off to grab the list of items for the liquor store, Liam turns to me.

"You ready to go?" For the first time ever, Liam's eyes scan the length of me.

Whether he's checking me out or simply seeing if I'm appropriately dressed so I won't embarrass him in public, I don't care. It's a milestone moment.

"Um," I glance down at my outfit. Not loving the vibe, I hold up a finger as I back toward the stairs. "I'll be ready in just a minute."

With Liam's nod, I rush up the stairs and into my room.

There, I stare into my closet in search of the perfect outfit that is put together without trying too hard. Something that matches Liam's style.

Embroidered flower cardigan?

Floral print overalls?

Vintage inspired fit and flare dress with bows on it?

Something from my collection of Peter Pan-collar blouses?

Normally my wardrobe makes me feel pretty and cozy, but nothing in this closet is going to impress Liam.

And now I'm having an anxious moment that if I change my clothes, it won't be an improvement and *that* will be more noticeable. Or worse, he won't notice at all, and I'll feel silly for changing in the first place.

I close my closet door and head to my bathroom to freshen up.

While I'm pulling out my deodorant, I grab my phone and call Cassie, putting it on speakerphone so I can use my hands.

"Change of plans. I can't hang out right now."

"What do you mean?" she shrieks. "I'm almost to your house."

I shut my bathroom door and press my back to it, trying to calm my heart rate. "Liam is here."

"Wait. THE Liam?" She sucks in a breath before letting it out in a squeal.

"Shh." I grab my phone and press the volume down. The last thing I need is for Liam to hear me gushing about him on this call. "And yes. THE Liam."

"Oh my god, I'm definitely coming over then."

"No, my mom asked me and Liam to go get wine for the party tonight. We're going to be alone, without Jasper since he's following Stella around like a lost puppy."

"You mean a horny puppy."

"Gross." I don't want to think about Jasper like that. "But, yeah."

I stretch the hem of my sweater out to make room for my deodorant stick, then switch sides to get the other armpit. I'm sweating buckets from the thought of being in an enclosed space with Liam so I'm not even sure a reapplication is going to help.

"Fine, I'll go home. But I'll be over later to get ready for the party."

"Sounds good," I say, applying some lip gloss before standing back to check my appearance. I should put on some foundation to cover up my freckles but there's no time.

"Juni?"

"Yeah?" I reply, pulling the top section of my hair back with a cream-colored bow scrunchie.

"Are you going to tell him how you feel?" she asks.

I swallow hard.

Tell Liam how I feel? I'm not delusional enough to think that I love him. Who falls in love with someone from afar? Do I even know him well enough to say that I'm crazy about him? Most of my information about Liam is second-hand or through stalking him on the internet. I can count the number of interactions we've had over the years on my fingers and toes, but each one has made my heart pound and my stomach flutter.

I'm certainly attracted to him. And knowing the company that Jasper keeps, Liam being his best friend and business partner means he's trustworthy.

"I don't know. Do you think I should?"

"You know what they say. Christmas is the best time to tell people how you feel about them."

"Who says that?"

"I think it was in a movie. You know, the one where the guy holds up the cards to tell his best friend's wife that he's been a jerk to her because he actually loves her."

"Yeah, but that scene was weird."

"You're right, but it's still a banger of a holiday movie."

"I don't know what I'm going to do. I'll just see what the vibes are."

"All right, fill me in later."

"Bye."

We end the call, and I pocket my phone before rushing downstairs to meet Liam.

# LIAM

"DO YOU LIKE MULLED WINE?" Juniper asks.

She moves ahead of me, scanning the shelves like she's on a mission. There's something focused in the way she moves—decisive, sharp—but every so often, she does this little bounce on her heels when she spots something she likes. I don't think she knows she does it.

It's strangely...endearing.

"What was the question?"

"Mulled wine. Are you a fan?" she asks, putting a bottle into the cart I'm pushing.

"Absolutely. I'll sell my soul for anything mulled this time of year."

She stops for a moment, staring up at me with a curious smile.

Beneath her overcoat, she's wearing a chunky cardigan sweater layered over a cropped tee, black leggings that hug her curves, and knit socks with a ruffle edge that peek out of her shearling trim lace-up boots.

And god, those freckles on her nose and cheeks. Maddeningly sexy. As if she wasn't distracting enough.

*Stop staring,* the voice in my head snaps at me. It's been loud ever since Juniper appeared at the door of her family's home a little over an hour ago.

I trail behind her in this tiny liquor store that smells like pine-scented candles and dust, trying to focus on the task but getting caught in her orbit instead.

I came to Cedar Hollow because I wanted something different this year. I told myself it was about needing a break, about checking in on Jasper. Making sure my best friend isn't too over his head with Stella, his childhood rival and the woman he's been obsessing over since I've known him. But now, watching Juniper pick out bottles with that fierce determination of hers, I realize it's more.

Maybe I came for what Jasper always had—a place to go back to. People who knew every version of him and still kept a seat at the table.

And maybe...it's because I want that, too.

But the weird flutter in my chest watching Juniper has me all fucked up.

This isn't June Bug anymore. That name, the childish nickname, doesn't fit the woman in front of me. I don't even know what fits. Or why the hell I can't stop staring at the soft cream silk bow that trails over the back of her copper hair.

At first glance, the bow is innocent. But the way the silk catches the light when she turns her head, it radiates femininity and confidence. It's graceful and elegant while taunting me in a way that begs for me to reach out and tug it.

"I think that's everything." She glances up, voice pulling me back.

"Good." I nod, pretending to be the executive in charge

of this shopping cart. Maybe business is the only place I can keep my head clear right now.

That's where I need to keep Juniper. In the business only category.

"Tell me about your bookshop," I say, steering the cart toward the register.

"Bookshop?" Juniper's brow creases for a moment, before it softens again. "I call it a bookstore, but I like bookshop better. It sounds more romantic." Those full pink lips of hers splay into a brilliant smile. "British accents have a way of doing that, I guess."

She's not the first woman to comment on my accent, but from Juniper it's endearing, not flirtatious. So then why am I still staring at her lips?

"What is it called?" I ask, pulling my eyes from her mouth.

"Blush & Binding." Her cheeks flush a little, the name rolling off her tongue like a secret.

"Blush because it's a romance bookshop?"

"And I love pink. It's going to have a pink door with a brass handle." She beams.

"And binding, because books are bound," I offer.

"Among other things," she says casually, a hint of a smirk playing at her lips.

I'm staring again. Looking at Jasper's little sister like she's a woman to be desired.

She's not.

I mean, she is, but not by me.

But fuck if she isn't gorgeous and so damn intriguing.

That is what is messing with my mind. I've only known Juniper as June Bug, the teenage version, and the woman standing in front of me is not her. It's a mind fuck seeing her this way. Standing close and inhaling her scent; sugar plum and sage. Wishing she weren't my best friend's little sister so I wouldn't feel guilty about leaning in closer and wondering what her lips would feel like on mine.

*Get ahold of yourself, Liam.* I can appreciate a woman and not do anything about it. I've done it plenty of times. I'm certain of it.

She picks up a bottle of peppermint liqueur from an endcap near the register. "Oh! We need this for the hot cocoa bar."

"Grand." The less I say, the better.

Suddenly, a woman approaches with a tray of tiny plastic cups filled with a creamy liquid.

"Would you like to try a sample?" she offers.

"What is it?" Juniper asks.

"Eggnog with anejo tequila." The employee hands us each a small plastic glass.

"Eggnog and tequila?" Juniper raises an eyebrow.

"Apparently." I examine the liquid in the cup, then smile at Juniper. "Let's give it a go."

"Cheers." Juniper clinks her cup against mine.

Our eyes lock as we sip. The nutty-flavored liquid slides down the back of my throat, the tequila giving it just enough warmth to heat my chest.

Juniper's eyes widen. "Oh, that's good."

I smile. "Yeah, it is."

We both laugh, the warmth of the tequila-laced eggnog spreading through more than just our limbs. Something shifts—just a little, but enough that the tension between us starts to unravel.

"We're tasting holiday drinks at the front," the woman says, "Eggnogs, whiskey ciders, and mulled wine, too."

Juniper's eyes light up. "You love mulled wine." She grabs my hand without thinking, like it's the most natural thing in the world. When her fingers, soft and warm, wrap around mine, a current zips through me so sharp I almost flinch. She probably doesn't even realize she's doing it, but I feel it everywhere.

I let her pull me to the front of the store where the woman with the samples is setting up another tasting.

At the sight of Juniper's enthusiasm, I force out a grin. "Careful. You keep handing me samples, I'll get tipsy and tell you all my secrets."

She tips her chin up, eyes sparkling with mischief. "I'm okay with that."

It knocks something loose in my chest. The way she says it, so easy, so sure. Like it's no big thing for someone to know all of me.

I don't think I've ever had that. Not really. Someone who'd want every hidden piece and wouldn't cringe at the prickly parts.

I swallow the thought before it can take root.

She turns to grab the next glass, but her gaze catches on the ink curling along my forearm. "How many tattoos do you have?"

I lift a brow. "Tattoos?"

She nods, eyes flicking to the one barely hidden under my sweater. "Like a dozen?"

"Depends on how you count them. Some blend together. Some I forget are even there." I pause, then smirk. "Why? You taking inventory?"

"I'm just curious," she says, tone light but her eyes still on mine. "They feel like stories. And you don't hand those out easily."

She's not wrong. I've known Juniper for years—my best friend's little sister, the one always hovering on the edge of the group, observant, quiet, bright—but this is the first time it's ever felt like we see each other. That she sees me.

And the worst part?

I want to let her.

"How about every drink you try, I'll show you a tattoo. Deal?"

She grins wide. "Deal. But fair warning, I'm tasting *everything*."

It shouldn't mean anything. We're two grown adults in a small-town liquor store tasting holiday samples, but the way she says everything curls around my ribs like a spark that won't go out.

I lean my hip against the tasting table, tipping my empty sample cup toward her. "All right then. Pick the next drink."

She grabs two tiny whiskey cider cups and hands me one. We clink them together, her pinky brushing mine. I down it, heat and cinnamon burning the back of my throat.

"Okay," she says, eyes bright. "Show me one."

I lift my left sleeve a few inches, turning my arm so she can see the black ink just inside my bicep. A simple compass tucked away so close you'd have to be let in to see it.

She steps closer to read the tiny letters, her head tilting to the side. The space between us shrinks, but I don't move. "This one?" I say, voice low. "Got it when I landed my first real investment deal. Meant to remind me not to lose my direction. Or my backbone."

She brushes a fingertip lightly over the lines. "Does it work?"

"Most days." I smile, even though my throat's tight. "Next?"

She presses another sample cup into my hand—spiced rum and cider this time.

When we set our cups down, I tug my collar down a bit to show her the small line of script near my collarbone. She leans in to read it, breath ghosting my throat. "What's it say?"

"'Only forward.'" My voice cracks a touch. "Same idea. No backtracking."

Her eyes flick to mine. "So, what's forward for you? After all the investor calls and quarterly reports, what's next?"

I hesitate. Nobody ever asks me that. Not like this. Not like they might actually care about the real answer.

"Don't tell Jasper," I say, tipping my cup toward her in mock warning. "But if I weren't tied up running numbers all day, I'd open a wine bar."

Her smile blooms so warm I feel it in my chest. "A wine bar?"

"Yeah." I look over at the shelves, the rows of dusty bottles. "Small, cozy. Good flights, pairings. A few quiet corners where people can come in and just...breathe. Maybe read. Talk. Fall in love."

She laughs softly, brushing my arm with her hand like it's the most normal thing. "Like a romance bookshop. But for wine."

"Exactly." I shrug, embarrassed at how much it means to say it out loud. "I guess it's silly."

"It's not silly." She says it so certain, so soft I almost lean in again. "It sounds perfect."

I clear my throat, forcing my eyes away from her mouth. "All right. One more sample?"

She smirks, handing me the last tasting cup. "One more tattoo, Hargrove."

I give her a look but lift my shirt anyway, just enough to show the slim line of ink under my ribs.

*So it goes.*

She squints, reading it, then her mouth curves. "Vonnegut?" she says, voice warm. "*Slaughterhouse-Five?*"

"Yeah." I grin, a little sheepish. "Not exactly festive, I know."

She shakes her head, eyes sparking with something I'm afraid to name. "It's perfect for you."

"Oh?" I arch a brow, fighting a laugh. "Why's that?"

Her teeth catch her bottom lip. "Because you're so buttoned up. But then you've got this secret little reminder that life's messy, and you're okay with it."

I huff a laugh, taking the tasting cup from her hand. "Secret's out, I guess."

She laughs, and for a second it's just us—the holiday chaos outside, the cold air waiting when we leave, none of it matters. Just her freckles, her warmth, and a hint of something that feels dangerously like home.

She nudges my side. "So...the CFO has a secret chaotic side."

I shrug. "Maybe. If the spreadsheets behave."

"Oh, that's why you'd open a wine bar." She grins, putting it together. "To lean into the chaos."

I tilt my head, pretending to think. "Or maybe I'd open a wine bar so certain girls could come drink mulled wine and boss me around."

She laughs, eyes catching on a display by the counter—cheap novelty pins and keychains. She plucks one up and holds it between two fingers, turning back to me with a sly grin.

"Here." She lifts it for me to see—a little red pin with *Spice It Up* in bold white letters. "This is so you."

I arch a brow. "Oh yeah?"

"A reminder," she says, faux serious, "for when you get too CFO about life."

I huff a laugh and roll my eyes. "You think I need reminding to be chaotic?"

She flashes a wicked smile. "Constantly."

She pretends to toss it into the basket with the bottles, but I'm already turning to help the clerk bag the wine and don't see what she does with it next.

When I glance back, her hands are empty. I shake my head at her, and she shrugs innocently, like it was just a joke.

We load the bags into the back, the sun already starting to dip behind the line of pines that guard the road back to her parents' house. She slides into the passenger seat, hugging her coat tighter, cheeks pink from the cold and the whiskey cider.

By the time I drop into the driver's seat, the radio kicks on. The mountain station is static for a moment, then a blast of old holiday pop. Wham!'s "Last Christmas." I reach to switch it off, but Juniper practically lunges over the console to slap my hand away.

"Don't you dare!" she gasps, half-laughing, half-scandalized. Her palm lands warm on my wrist.

"Wham!?" I tilt my head, grinning at her outrage. "Of all the classics, you choose this?"

She levels me with a look, like I've just insulted the queen. "It's iconic," she insists. "It's heartbreak and hope and drama. Also, that video? Pure eighties chaos. George Michael in a holiday sweater? Top-tier Christmas content."

Her eyes light up. "Plus, it's set at a wintry mountain

cabin. I mean, that's basically Cedar Hollow, right? Snow, ski lifts, pine trees…it's cozy and cold and perfect."

I huff a laugh, shaking my head as I pull out onto Founders Street. "I stand by it. "Fairytale of New York" is better."

She gasps. "Oh my god. That song is so depressing!"

"It's honest."

"Grinch." She flicks my arm playfully.

I shoot her a sideways look. "You know, I never took you for a cheesy Christmas pop girl."

She crosses her arms, mock-offended, then breaks into a grin. "You don't know me at all, Liam Hargrove."

No. I don't. But god, I want to.

The song croons on, and Juniper's quiet humming weaves around the chorus like she's done this a thousand times.

When the last note fades out, the silence hits warmer than before.

I pull the car into the Jensens' driveway and drop it into park before turning my attention to her again.

"This is…" I trail off, the words evaporating from my brain before I can get them out.

"What?" She laughs.

Fuck, that laugh of hers is magic. It bubbles up and wraps around my ribs. And for one sharp heartbeat, I want it—her—so badly it terrifies me.

"It's—we've never talked like this before."

Her face lights up, and I'm wondering what the hell I'm getting myself into.

"It's fun, right?"

I reach out to finger a shorter piece of hair that has fallen across her face.

My eyes fall to her lips. I don't mean for them to. It's

that damn tequila eggnog or the whiskey cider, or fuck, maybe it's just *her*.

The passenger door opens and at Jasper's appearance, I drop my hand.

"How'd the liquor run go?" he asks.

"Great!" Juniper gives me a brilliant smile before hopping out of the vehicle. "Gotta get ready. See you later?"

"Yeah," I answer, though inside I'm suddenly hyper-aware of exactly who she is and what that means.

# JUNIPER

AFTER MY TIME with Liam at the liquor store, I'd come home more hopeful than ever. Hopeful that maybe, just maybe, he saw me. Not just as Jasper's little sister, but as me.

Cassie and I got ready in my room, then came down to help finish setting up for the party.

I'm fussing with the hot cocoa bar when Stella appears beside me in an emerald green dress that looks unfairly gorgeous on her.

She's one of those women who makes everything look easy. Like she was born with a blow dryer in one hand and a Pinterest board in the other. She's the creative director at East & Ivy for a reason.

"You look stunning," she says, pulling me in for a warm hug. I've always admired Stella and seeing her with Jasper makes my romance-loving heart do cartwheels. He's been half in love with her forever. I just hope she doesn't break him.

"Thanks. You do, too." I smile.

She glances around. "Do you have a date tonight?"

"No, I'm keeping my options open." I do my best to sound casual, but my eyes snag on Liam standing across the room talking with a group of neighbors. He looks devastating in a dark green quarter-zip sweater and fitted charcoal pants. Relaxed. Confident. Completely out of my league.

He hasn't looked at me since I came downstairs, and that has me analyzing every second of our interaction at the liquor store. Maybe it was the tequila eggnog making me think he was flirting. Or maybe I've spent too much time reading about romance and I can't identify when a guy is actually flirting with me. But I swear on Jane Austen's ghost, Liam was flirting with me.

I'm still spiraling when a quiet voice cuts through the noise.

"Hey, Juniper."

I turn and there he is. Right beside me. His nearness and that low, warm voice settle every flailing thought.

"Merry Christmas Eve," he says, and we clink our glasses together.

My arm moves on autopilot while my brain scrambles for something—anything—smart to say.

*What do you think happens to the Christmas ornaments that don't get sold each year?*

*Would you rather fight one reindeer-sized elf or ten elf-sized reindeer?*

*Have you ever smelled a book so good you questioned your life choices?*

But all I manage is a breathless smile.

"I've been thinking about your bookshop since we talked earlier," he says.

"Oh, yeah?" My chaotic brain quiets at the thought of talking about my absolute most favorite thing.

"Jasper mentioned you won't take on investors."

I shake my head. "Nope. I want it to be mine. But I'm applying for a local business grant." The thought twists my stomach. My half-done business plan flashes behind my eyes like a crime scene.

"What's that face?" he asks, amused.

"It's the 'I'm-doomed-and-don't-want-to-admit-it' face." I sigh. "The grant requires a business plan and I'm...stuck."

His smile does something catastrophic to my insides. "Show it to me."

I press my lips together, hating the idea of showing him the messy proposal I'm working on. "It's not finished."

"Perfect." He grins. "Let me help."

"It's Christmas Eve, Liam. That's not what you want to be doing."

"It's fun for me." He says it so simply, so easily, that my heart does a traitorous little somersault. "Come on, I want to see it."

I imagine Liam begging me to see something else, and it makes my legs quiver.

The intensity of his stare has my temperature spiking.

"Okay." I nod, gesturing toward the stairs. "It's in my room."

He motions for me to lead the way. As we ascend the stairs, I send a silent thank you to Cassie for helping me hide the tornado we left behind while getting ready. Still, there's something mortifying about stepping into my childhood bedroom with Liam.

When we enter, he sits down on my bed, all casual confidence, like the sight of him there doesn't have my heart skittering against my ribs. I dig the folder from my desk drawer, then drop down beside him. Our knees brush, and I pretend not to notice how his thigh feels solid and warm against mine.

He flips through the pages; brow furrowed in concentration. I can barely look at him. The air fills thick with something I don't know how to name.

"Juniper, this isn't terrible," he murmurs, "but your numbers don't add up. Where's your cash flow projection?" He flips a page. "You haven't accounted for marketing expenses at all."

"You mean businesses don't run on optimism and vibes alone?" I say dryly, but my voice wobbles.

He smiles, slow and soft, and it does something catastrophic to my pulse. "They do once a good business plan is in place."

Overwhelmed, I drop my face into my hands. The nerves. The pressure. The fact that Liam Hargrove is sitting on my bed and I'm trying to pretend that I'm not thinking about how kissable his mouth looks.

A moment later, gentle fingers wrap around my wrist, coaxing my hands away.

"Hey." His voice is low, the word rough at the edges.

I look up and instantly regret it. He's so close. His thigh flush against mine. His hand still holding my wrist. His aftershave smells like cedar and cloves, and there's cinnamon on his breath from the whiskey cider he's been drinking.

"We'll figure it out," he says, voice low and sure. "I'll help you."

Something tight and breathless unfurls inside me.

"Okay," I whisper, already forgetting what we were talking about because all I can see is him and how close his mouth is. Because he's looking at me like I matter. Like he wants—

"Juniper."

His voice vibrates through me. My tongue darts out to wet my lips. His eyes drop, tracking it. On a sharp inhale, his fingers tighten around my wrist like he's deciding whether to pull me in.

This is it.

The moment I've been afraid to hope for, right in front of me.

Before I lose my nerve, I lean forward and kiss him.

For one sweet heartbeat, the world stops. Liam's lips are soft but firm, tasting like cinnamon and heat and something I want more of.

And then...he kisses me back. Harder than I expected. Like he means it. Like he wants it, too.

His free hand cups my jaw, his thumb grazing my cheek as a low, desperate sound rumbles from his chest. It's relief and need and passion, and it breaks me open in the best way.

I sigh into his mouth, knees pressed tight to his thigh. I want more. I want all of him.

Our kiss becomes more frantic, and I move to straddle him. My skirt rides up my tight-clad legs, and I'm barely aware of the sound of paper—my business plan—falling to the floor. I don't care. All I care about is the way he's holding me like he can't help himself.

"Juniper..." His voice is rough against my lips.

"Hmm?"

He kisses me again, slower, deeper, like he wants to memorize my taste. Then he pulls back just enough to look at me. There's a look in his eyes I can't place—part longing, part panic.

"That was...unexpected," he says with a smile that doesn't quite reach his eyes. But we're here and this moment won't recreate itself, so I go all in.

"Liam, I want you to be my first."

He blinks. "First...what?"

"Sex." I force the word out, barely more than a whisper. "I want it to be you."

He goes completely still beneath me, then his hands drop away like I burned him. The warmth in his face drains.

"Wait—what?" His voice is hoarse.

"I've thought about it for a long time," I rush on. "I trust you. I want it to be—"

"No." The word cuts through me like a blade. "Juniper, no. That's...no."

He shifts beneath me, trying to stand, and in the scramble, I lose my balance and land hard on the floor with a yelp.

"Shit—" He drops down beside me instantly, his hands on my hips to steady me.

But I'm not steady. I'm falling apart. And my heart is pounding for all the wrong reasons now.

"I didn't mean to..." He drags a hand through his hair. "God, I shouldn't have—I got caught up and—Juniper, I didn't know that's what this was."

"Why not?" I hate how fragile my voice sounds. "Why can't it be me?"

He doesn't answer right away, just stares at the floor like it holds a map out of this mess.

"Because you're—" he pauses. "You're Jasper's sister. And I'm older. And this isn't how it should happen for you."

"We're six years apart, not sixty," I snap, trying to salvage my pride, even as my face burns. "You kissed me back," I whisper, clinging to the memory of Liam's lips pressing hard into mine.

He looks tortured. "Yeah. And that was my mistake."

His words hit like a slap.

"Right," I say, swallowing hard as I push his hands off my hips and crawl to my feet. "Well. Thanks for your help."

"Juniper—wait—"

But I'm already rushing for the door, head high, chest splintering open with every step.

# THIS CHRISTMAS

# ONE
## JUNIPER

I PLACE the last ornament on the tree in the window and step back to take it in. Pink satin bows, white sparkly snowflakes, and an assortment of mini book ornaments that I made at the crafting class I hosted last week. The tree goes perfectly with the pink and white themed décor of Blush & Binding, Cedar Hollow's romance-only bookstore—my dream.

My store has been open six months, and I'm beyond excited to be celebrating its first holiday season. Romance books and the holidays are two of my loves, so putting them together is absolute magic.

In addition to the tree, I've decked the entire store out in festive holiday décor. The strands of greenery are the perfect complement to the pink scalloped-top bookshelves, while the twinkle lights framing the shelves give that cozy, warm glow.

I grab the extra box of ornaments and carry it over to the storage bin for safe keeping. When I pass the south wall of bookshelves, I let my fingers skim along a step of the sliding ladder. A handful of months later, and I'm still obsessed with it. It's exactly the kind of detail I used to dream about, curled up with a romance novel and a mug of tea. Sometimes, when the store's empty, I hop on and slide from one end to the other just because I can.

It's a vision come to life. Exactly how I imagined it since I knew I wanted to open a romance-only bookstore.

But no matter how beautiful it looks, I can't stop the way the twinkling lights and familiar scent of warm vanilla chai with hints of fir balsam and cinnamon unearth the memories of last Christmas. Of Liam, and his rejection.

*But Liam is a chapter I've already closed,* I remind myself.

I have the receipts—college degree, signed lease, dream career, and a thriving book club. And the business plan that I worked diligently on in order to receive the small-business grant from the Cedar Hollow Chamber of Commerce.

As it turns out, I didn't need Liam's help because I joined the Summit County Small-Business forum and it's been a wealth of information. One particular member, *PourChoices*, has given me a lot of good advice with budget and marketing, both not being strong suits of mine.

So, I refuse to let some nostalgic scent pull me back into the depths of humiliation that Liam's rejection had written into my story, like a cruel plot twist I never saw coming.

I'm just about to mentally rewrite that scene with a more satisfying ending—maybe one that puts my bookstore ladder to good use—when the bell jingles over the door, tugging me back to the present.

Its melodic ring is my favorite sound in the store. Second only to the soft turning of pages as customers nestled in my cozy reading nook lose themselves in their latest bookish escape.

"I'll be right with you," I call cheerily. Even though the

store closes in five minutes, I want every customer to have a top-notch experience.

I finish unpacking the last few books from the box. It's Pippa Monroe's latest bestseller, and though I've already read it, I set a copy aside for myself to purchase later and place on my bookshelf at home.

"Welcome to Blush & Binding," I say, approaching the man who just walked in. "How can I—" He turns toward me, revealing his chiseled cheekbones and warm smile. My words falter, and I stop dead in my tracks.

Standing there is Liam Hargrove, and he looks even more devilishly handsome than I remember.

My eyes drift over him, hungry for every detail.

He's wearing a black wool coat, and his hair is dusted by the snowflakes falling outside. Also in place, a smug, cheerful smile.

I promised myself last Christmas was the last time Liam Hargrove would leave me feeling like an idiot. And yet here I am, twelve months later, my heart tripping over itself as he walks through the front door of my bookstore like he owns the air.

He glances around, taking in my store, and I hate that I care what he thinks about it.

"Hey, Juniper." His accent wraps around me like the opening lines of a book I swore I'd never reread. And when he smiles at me, my heart pounds so loud, I can hear it in my ears. "You did it. And it's bloody brilliant."

My swoony, romance-loving heart wants to stay in this state forever, but all it takes is one instant replay of the night when Liam kissed me like I was his, then rejected me, to scatter all those feelings.

"What are you doing here?" I ask, not bothering to hide the suspicion in my voice. "Because unless you're looking for a signed copy of *Billionaire's Christmas Baby Pact*, I can't imagine what would bring you in."

Liam doesn't miss a beat. "I already have that one."

I blink, my brain immediately trying to picture Liam lounging on his couch reading a spicy holiday romance.

His mouth curves into a grin. "E-book and paperback. Don't judge me."

"Oh, I'm judging you," I say, though it comes out shakier than I mean. "Next thing you'll tell me you're in a romance book club."

He shrugs, his long fingers dancing over the top of a paperback on the display table. "Maybe I am."

I gape at him.

He gestures toward the table of holiday releases. "You think I'd come back here unprepared?"

"Unprepared for what?"

His eyes lift to mine, but he doesn't respond. I hate that part of me hopes it's for me. That he's back because he regrets everything.

But that doesn't matter, because I can't go back to being the girl with the silly crush. I refuse to be in that position again.

Liam's mouth opens to speak, but the door jingles again, pulling our attention to it. Walking toward us, beaming and snow-dusted, are Stella and Jasper.

"You're not going to believe this," Stella says, flashing a diamond ring.

"We're engaged!" Jasper grins.

Before his words are out, I'm leaping at Stella. I wrap her up in a hug before pulling back to admire her ring. I'm aware that Liam is congratulating Jasper with a hug before we exchange positions and I embrace my big brother.

"Congratulations!" I shriek with delight in Jasper's ear.

"Thanks, Juni."

When Jasper releases me, I go back to admiring Stella's ring and asking all the details of how it happened.

"And then," Stella says, "I pulled out the ring I got for him."

"You were planning to propose, too?!" I exclaim, taking in the sight of a ring on Jasper's finger as well.

I gape at them with a beaming smile, but when I feel Liam staring at me, I scowl and throw him some side eye. He smiles back at me, that crooked grin of his making my insides turn to mush.

I ignore it—and him—and turn back to talking with Jasper and Stella while Liam quietly listens.

The bell above the door jingles again and this time it's my mom. I laugh when I see that she's carrying champagne and glasses. Clearly, she couldn't wait for the engagement news to come to her.

"A little birdie told me we have something to celebrate." When her eyes land on Liam, they light up. "Oh, my goodness. Liam, I didn't know you were in town."

My mom embraces him and a pang of jealousy ripples through my veins. Because what would it be like to hug that man casually and feel nothing?

He shrugs but smiles at Jasper and Stella. "I couldn't miss the big event."

It hits me that Jasper must have shared his intention to propose to Stella with Liam, and that's why he's here. To celebrate Stella and Jasper's engagement.

It makes far more sense than the idea that he might have arrived in our small, mountain town for other reasons that shall not be named, because I'm done with that silliness.

But the disappointment that causes my belly to dip is a reminder that clearly my feelings for Liam haven't fizzled out like I'd hoped. God, I hate that he still affects me. That time hasn't healed this wound.

"Well, Liam, we're happy to have you here."

I can't help the snort of derision that leaves my nasal cavity, but when everyone turns to stare at me, I cover it up with a cough. "I've been fighting this cold." My fingers tap my chest to emphasize my fake upper respiratory struggle.

"Have you been using that humidifier I gave you?" my mom asks sincerely. "It's a must with this dry winter air."

"I'll get right on that."

My mom pops open the champagne, then hands each of us a glass. I take mine and down it, hoping the bubbles will lift me out of this awkward situation.

"Liam, where are you staying?" my mom asks.

I set down the champagne glass and focus on reorganizing the books on the front holiday themed table. I already did it earlier, but I need a distraction, so I mindlessly do it again.

"I don't have lodging yet."

My mom's eyes widen with panic. "We've got family and guests coming in from all over this year. My mother-in-law will be staying with us, and we've got Jasper and Juniper's cousins and their new baby."

Jasper nods. "We're staying with Stella's family, but it's a full house there as well."

"No problem. I'm sure I can book a room at the inn like I did last year."

"Oh no," my mom gasps, "I hate to say, I already spoke to Mildred at the Snowshoe Inn. It's completely booked through New Year's."

"Oh." Liam's grin drops a notch. His eyes shift to me, but I cross my arms and glance away. I've got no sympathy.

Should have planned ahead, *buddy*.

"What about a vacation rental?" Jasper suggests. "I could have Janelle at the office book something for you."

"I already had her check for the cabin you rented last year, and everything is booked up," Stella adds.

"Oh no. I guess he can't stay." I widen my eyes, my fake worry so sweet I almost gag on it.

"What about your place, June Bug?" my mom says brightly, like she's just dropped the last piece into a thousand-piece puzzle we've been working on for days.

My heart rate kicks into high gear.

My jaw drops.

"Mom—"

She steamrolls my protest. "It's perfect! We just finished setting up her guest room. It has new bedding and the coziest reading nook."

"I'm sure that's exactly what Liam needs—a cozy reading nook," Jasper teases.

When my eyes meet Liam's, I silently scream a warning: *Say. No.*

But he ignores my plea and that stupid, devastating smile curves his mouth.

"I'd be honored to be Juniper's first guest."

His eyes find mine, sparking with something I can't name and definitely don't trust.

Well, fan-fucking-tastic. The man who humiliated me last Christmas is now sleeping down the hall. And I'm supposed to play nice? Pretend like nothing happened?

Oh, ho ho, hell no.

I STAND behind Juniper on the stairs, waiting for her to unlock the door to her flat above her bookshop. It's a narrow space, but I don't mind. Standing this close, I can smell her—something soft and floral, like jasmine and winter air. And something sweet, like plums.

I need a moment to look at her. With her defensive edge and everyone else around earlier, I hadn't been able to stare at her openly.

Damn. She's a sight for sore eyes.

I've seen her photos online. Followed her updates. Watched from afar as she built Blush & Binding from scratch and documented every milestone.

Her copper hair is pinned back with one of those silky bows I find fascinating, loose tendrils framing her face. Her fuzzy pink sweater makes her look like a valentine. Soft and warm. The look she gives me over her shoulder is not.

"Just so you know, you're not my first guest," she says as she jiggles the key in the lock. "I've had other guests. Male ones. Lots of them."

*Bloody hell.*

My jaw tenses at the thought of Juniper with another man.

She seems overly excited to share that information so it could be a bluff. But from the sight of her, the way she carries herself as a woman and business owner, there's no doubt in my mind she could have any guy she wanted.

Last year, she wanted me, but I fucked it up. Too shocked by the discovery that I was having feelings for my best friend's sister to properly react to her advances.

She doesn't owe me anything, but that doesn't stop the pang in my chest.

If she's no longer a virgin, I hope it was with someone who saw her properly. Not some tosser who didn't know how lucky he was.

"Noted," I respond, in an effort to calm the jealous rage inside of me.

She gets the door open and steps into the flat. But then she turns suddenly, and now we're wedged together in the tight hallway.

Our breath mingles.

Her eyes find my lips.

My restraint thins.

I debate kissing her right now and telling her all my regrets. But one wrong move and I could ruin everything I came here to fix.

She steps away first, putting space between us.

"Don't worry, Hargrove," she says coolly, "the crush is long gone. You're just a houseguest now."

Her words slice clean through my ribs.

"Oh, and you were right last year. That kiss was a mistake."

I study her, head to toe. Taking note of the way her

chest rises and falls unevenly. She's lying. Maybe to herself more than to me.

"Was it?" I counter.

She hesitates, like she's forgotten her line in a rehearsed script. "Uh, yeah."

A hard swallow makes its way down her slender neck. My fingers twitch at the vivid memory of her pulse beneath them. It feels like no time has passed. Like that kiss lives under my skin, waiting.

I want to lay it all out for her now, every reason I'm here, what I want from her, from us. But she's not ready. I can see it in her stiff shoulders, the tight line of her mouth. If I push too hard now, I'll lose any ground I've got.

Patience. Stick to the plan.

She spins away, releasing the tension between us.

"This is my apartment. Oh, I mean my *flat*," she says, sweetly acidic.

My brows tick up. "I see we're mocking the accent now."

"Just helping you translate." She flashes me a feisty smirk.

She's cheeky as hell, and I love it.

"Coat closet." She motions to the door just inside her flat before slipping off her boots and walking away. I remove my coat and open the closet door. Inside, I find Juniper's coats hanging in a neat row, her scent clinging to the fabric —warm, familiar, and impossible to resist. I hang my coat alongside hers and hope that her scent will weave its way into the material.

After closing the closet door, I remove my boots and leave them neatly next to Juniper's before wandering into her flat.

A plush, floral rug covers the wooden floor of the

hallway while a small sage green side table sits beneath a scalloped-edge gold-framed mirror.

The living room is centered around a velvet loveseat in blush and a vintage-style, oriental print area rug in complementing colors. White bookshelves filled with books, as if it's an extension of her bookstore, along with a few plants, candles, and trinkets. One wall has a framed gallery. Some frames have art prints, others dried flowers and lyrical quotes. A gold bar cart sits beneath the frames with rose gold glassware and a few bottles of spirits.

A wooden calendar hangs on the wall near her kitchen, shaped like a gingerbread house, with tiny hand-painted doors, each labeled with a glittery number. One is slightly ajar, revealing a packet of hot cocoa and a slip of folded paper.

"What's this?" I ask, lifting a hand to peek inside.

Before I can, she's there, slamming it shut. "It's my advent calendar."

"You made it?"

"Yes." She says it like a dare.

Even in her attempt to keep me at arm's length, I see the pride she has in it.

"And you filled it yourself?"

"Of course. Who else would know what I like?"

Her head tilts upward, giving me the perfect view of her features. The smattering of freckles on her nose and cheeks, her warm hazel eyes, and those perfect pink lips.

*Who else, indeed.*

Our gazes lock for the briefest of moments before she looks away.

She clears her throat, flustered. "Living room, kitchen." She motions quickly to the strikingly decorated rooms before turning and heading down the hallway. "Bedrooms are this way."

My gaze returns to the gingerbread house advent calendar.

It's something she's poured time into. Something meant to make every day feel like a celebration. I desperately want to know what is behind each door. All of Juniper's favorite things.

But instead, I grab my luggage and follow her down the hallway. She stops in front of an open door.

"Guest bedroom is here." She motions across the hall. "Bathroom's there. It's the only one."

My eyes flick to the door next to the guest room. "Yours, I presume?"

Her arms cross against her chest. "Yeah."

It's like she's recalling the last time I was in her room. Her childhood bedroom where I'd reviewed her business plan, kissed her, then panicked.

"I'll let you get settled." She turns to reach for the handle on her bedroom door.

"Juniper?"

"What?" she asks, not bothering to turn around.

I want to say it all. Tell her what she doesn't know, what I'm about to do for us both. But she's not ready for my whole hand yet. So, I give her a single truth instead.

"That kiss wasn't a mistake. It was a revelation. That's why it scared the bloody hell out of me."

Her back goes rigid. For half a heartbeat I think she might turn and give me something. An opening, a sign. But she doesn't. Instead, she walks in her bedroom and closes the door.

Good. Let her be mad.

I'm not here for her approval.

I'm here to win her back. On my terms. One step at a time.

And this time, I won't fuck it up.

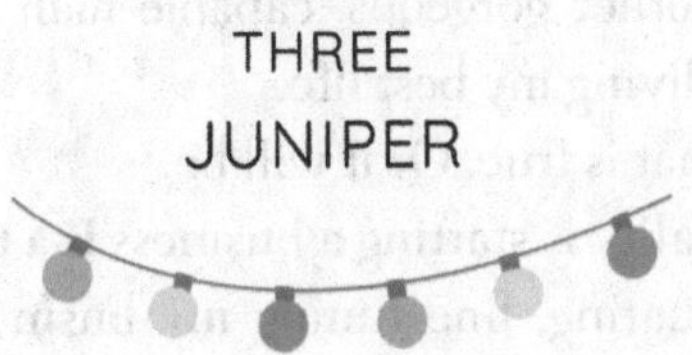

# THREE
# JUNIPER

LIAM'S WORDS echo in my head.

I can't remember the exact order of them, but a few stuck.

*Wasn't a mistake.*

*Revelation.*

*Scared.*

At his words, I'd wanted to turn and ask a million questions, but my bruised heart—and ego—wouldn't let me. Liam may have regrets but that doesn't mean he wants anything from me now.

From the moment he stood outside my apartment—hell, from the moment he walked into Blush & Binding—I've been trying to play it cool. And I feel like I'm failing.

The erratic apartment tour I just gave him made me feel like I was hosting a real estate show on fast-forward before leaving him and his suitcase outside my guest room and bolting into my bedroom.

This was not on my bingo card. I know because I hand-made all the bingo cards for the Books & Bubbly event next week, and *crush who humiliated you last Christmas confesses kiss wasn't a mistake* was not on it.

While my virginity is still intact, I want Liam to think that after he rejected me, I didn't skip a beat. I'd gone out and found another gorgeous, capable man to do the deed. And now I'm living my best life.

Some of that is true. Or it will be.

But the reality is starting a business is a ton of work, and between graduating, fine tuning my business plan for the grant submission, and then finally getting the bookstore underway, I've had no time for a personal life.

Liam doesn't need to know that.

My phone buzzes in my pocket and I realize while I was playing tour guide, I missed messages from the group chat.

CASSIE

Merry Moose tonight

WILEY

Is that different from any other night?

CASSIE

Yeah, there will be more interesting people to look at.

WILEY

But you're going to be there

CASSIE

Fuck off, Wy

WILEY

Ladies first

CASSIE

Three is starting to be a crowd.

Cassie and Wiley have a thing. They flirt, they bicker, they make out, then regret it in the morning. Rinse and repeat. Right now, I'd take any third-wheel drama over the hot-and-cold tension humming between Liam and me.

I type back that I'll meet them at The Merry Moose in twenty minutes, then rummage through my closet until I find my cream sweater dress. I cinch it with a belt, pull on my fleece-lined tights, then zip up my stiletto boots. The boots are impractical for snow, but practicality went out the window the second Liam Hargrove moved in for the holidays.

If he wants to lurk in my apartment, fine. But he can watch me walk out of it looking so good he chokes on his own regret. I'm in full-on *Eat your heart out, Liam Hargrove* mode.

In my bathroom mirror, I touch up my curls, swipe on some lip gloss, and force my heartbeat into a normal cadence. I can do this. I can survive him. I can win this silent standoff.

I march down the hallway, then reach for my coat in the closet.

"Where are you off to?" Liam's voice rolls over my shoulder.

I spin and find him hunched over my kitchen table, sleeves rolled up, reading *Business Journal*. He looks like a man who could buy and sell entire companies before breakfast—and then ruin your life after dark, just for fun.

But all I can see is last Christmas, the way he sat on my childhood bed, flipping through my half-baked business plan—pointing out projections and missed expenses—then kissed me like he wanted to ruin me for anyone else.

And now he's sitting here, in my kitchen, looking at me like he might do it again.

*Not happening*, I remind myself.

"The Merry Moose," I say, trying to sound breezy.

He folds up the paper, slow as ever, and moves to stand. "I'll come with you."

The thought of Liam hovering beside me at The Merry Moose while I try to drown the tension between us in a whiskey-spiked eggnog is not the vibe I was going for tonight.

And that's when it really sinks in. He's not just crashing in my guest room. He's going to be everywhere for the next few weeks. Haunting Cedar Hollow like a ghost of Christmas past. Hanging around my parents' house like he belongs there. Slipping right back into our holiday traditions like he didn't leave a kiss-shaped rejection lodged in my chest. And I'll have to slap on a self-assured grin and pretend like I don't feel it every time I look at him.

That I don't remember the humiliation. The heart ache. And what I can only imagine he felt for me...pity.

Well, not if I have anything to say about it.

"I have a date," I announce, the words tumbling out before I can second-guess myself. My subconscious clearly wants me to survive this with my dignity intact. By any means necessary.

Liam's eyes narrow. "With whom?"

"That's none of your concern."

He's quiet for a moment, and just when I think he's not going to push me on it, his lips curve into a maddening smile.

"I'll grab my coat."

If Liam knows I'm lying about the date, he doesn't let on as we make our way downstairs.

One of the perks of my apartment being located above

Blush & Binding is living in the heart of downtown Cedar Hollow, surrounded by shops, restaurants, and cozy cafés strung with twinkle lights year-round.

Liam nods toward the construction site next door. It used to be Wild Fern but after expanding, the owners moved operations to a greenhouse out near The Frosty Fir Tree Farm. The storefront sat empty for a few months, which wasn't great for a new business trying to draw foot traffic, but I'm hopeful about the incoming tenant.

"What do we have here?" Liam asks.

"It's going to be a wine bar."

Liam grins. "A perfect neighbor for your bookshop."

"I know." For a moment, my guard drops, and I can't help but smile.

Last Christmas, he'd mentioned that if he ever quit the CFO grind, he'd want to open a wine bar. Somewhere cozy, with wine flights and good music. A place to unwind. To fall in love. I hadn't thought about that conversation in months. Not until now.

"It seems someone else is living your dream."

He glances at me, a hint of something unreadable in his eyes. "Maybe. But some dreams change." His smile softens. "Honestly, just being neighbors with you would be a dream in itself."

The comment makes my pulse stutter. I'm not sure if he's flirting or just being nice, but either way, my face is warm.

I force my attention back to the fact that I still haven't met the wine bar owner in person, but we've chatted through the Summit County Small-Business forum and even discussed potential collaborations. The owner, whose handle in the forum is *PourChoices*, has been a helpful resource for our small-town businesses, but especially me. A few months ago, he reviewed my marketing plan and gave me tips on cutting overhead costs.

I'm curious who the owner is, but even Robyn down at the chamber of commerce has been cagey about their identity.

I'm half tempted to open the forum and message the elusive business owner for advice on what to do when your very inconvenient houseguest is your brother's best friend slash walking heartbreak. But that's ridiculous. And I'd never admit how much I rely on a stranger's encouragement.

We're halfway down Founders Street, walking toward The Merry Moose when my heel skids on a patch of ice. Instinctively, I reach out, grabbing Liam's arm for balance.

His hand covers mine and that zap of electricity I always feel from him hits me.

"Interesting choice of footwear," he murmurs, studying me.

I ignore the way his gaze lingers, how his brow arches just enough to make me feel like he's onto my plan to drive him wild and he's not falling for it.

"They're festive," I say, lifting my chin.

My boots are black, snug at the ankle, with stiletto heels that click against the pavement like a warning. Tiny gold rhinestones catch the streetlight with every step, like I'm walking in a constellation. They're completely impractical, wildly dramatic, and exactly the energy I need tonight.

"Functional, too. Especially on ice."

I keep my eyes forward, determined not to take the bait.

What does he know, anyway? Just because he looks like he walked out of a ski lodge catalog in that perfectly fitted coat and those smugly appropriate boots doesn't mean he gets to judge my footwear. Even if they are completely impractical.

Still, I can feel the warmth of his gaze on me. And I hate how aware of him I am—of the way his arm felt when I grabbed it, steady and solid like it was the most natural thing in the world. I hate even more how part of me wants to slip again just so I can touch him.

He doesn't say anything else, but the amused glint in his eye lingers as we continue walking.

And yeah, I'm starting to think he is on to me.

The moment I open the door to The Merry Moose, I'm greeted with a burst of warm air. As we enter, there's a mix of chatter and laughter from the packed tables, with the classic "Rockin' Around the Christmas Tree" blaring over the sound system.

Liam glances around the space, taking in the glittering ornaments hanging from the ceiling, the festive twinkle light garland decorating the rustic mahogany bar, and of course the sprig of mistletoe dangling from the wooden beam between the arcade room and the front of the bar that was the catalyst for Stella and Jasper's first kiss last year.

And now they're engaged.

My heart wants to linger on the romance of it all, but I need a plan. And fast.

The benefit to Liam not being a local is I could pretty much pass anyone off as my date without him suspecting. I scan the bar looking for a potential fake date.

My eyes land on Wiley. He's across the bar sipping on a Nutcracker Stout, his favorite beer. He lives for that shit.

By a stroke of luck, Wiley sees me coming and smiles.

"How's my best girl, Juni Petuni?" he croons, grabbing my hand to spin me around.

He's probably three beers in, but he's the best I've got.

"Pretend we're on a date," I rush out, knowing Liam isn't far behind.

Wiley scrunches his nose. "Really? I was hoping to get that blonde's number." He gestures to a woman near the bar.

"Pretend now and I'll be your wing woman later."

He quirks his lips and bobs his head side to side like he's really thinking about it.

"I'm the best wing woman and you know it." I press a finger into his chest for emphasis.

"Fine," he sighs. "What do I have to do?"

I glance around, relieved that Liam didn't follow me. Instead, I find him talking nearby with Jasper and Stella. They're surrounded by a group of people congratulating them on their engagement. I should go over and talk to them, but I desperately want to keep my distance from Liam.

"Pretend I'm irresistible. Especially when the man in the burgundy sweater is around."

Wiley glances in Liam's direction, then awkwardly puts an arm over my shoulders. Trying to appear flirtatious, I start laughing loudly.

"Why are you laughing?" Wiley asks.

"Because you told a joke."

"No, I didn't."

I groan but do my best to keep a smile on my face. "Wiley, you are so bad at this."

"Pretending is not my strong suit."

"Is that why the women you sleep with hate you the next morning? You can't even pretend to care about them?"

"Ouch."

"The truth hurts. Ask Lizzo." I shrug, then glance around. "Where's Cass?"

"Playing some tourist at darts."

That sounds about right.

"I'm going to get a drink," I say, turning to head toward the bar. Then I pause, glancing back at Wiley. "Hey, I need you fully committed to this. Are you in?"

He takes a sip of his beer casually. "Yeah, definitely." His eyes flick to the basketball game on the screen. "Also, grab me another beer?"

I narrow my eyes. "Wiley."

He finally looks at me, and I step forward, rising on my toes to press a quick kiss to his cheek. At the contact of my lips, he flinches.

"I didn't think kissing was part of the deal."

I shoot him a pointed look. "Play the part."

His shoulders straighten. "Right. Got it."

Then, loudly enough for half the bar to hear: "All right, baby, see you in a few."

I sigh, biting back a groan, but then I offer him a quick smile. This is Wiley trying.

# FOUR
# LIAM

"SO, WHAT'S THE PLAN?" Stella asks, finally getting a moment of reprieve from all the well-wishers congratulating her and Jasper on their engagement.

"I'm not certain. I hadn't anticipated competition."

"Oh?" She arches a brow. "Is that because you didn't realize my future sister-in-law is not only gorgeous, brilliant, and a savvy businesswoman, but such a catch she's not waiting around for the man who rejected her last Christmas?"

At his fiancée's snarky reply, my best friend's eyebrows lift in amusement.

Jasper and Stella already know how I feel about Juniper. Back around Thanksgiving, when Jasper pulled me aside to show me the ring he'd bought Stella, I'd congratulated him, then promptly confessed about Juniper. About the kiss, at least. The rest of that night is something I'll keep between me and her.

Our conversation was when I finally admitted out loud that I was done pretending my feelings weren't real.

Jasper likes to joke that I needed a road map to my own

feelings, but at least I'm not waiting twenty years like he did.

My glare sharpens. "Every man should drop to their knees in front of Juniper." Then quieter, more certain, "But I'm the one who'll earn the right to stay there."

Jasper's eyes darken. "Didn't we make a pact? No references to being on your knees for my sister. Ever."

I huff a dry laugh, but don't take the bait. There's something more important I need to know. I turn to Jasper. "What did you do last year when Stella's former fling was sniffing around?"

Jasper chuckles. "Daniel was no competition."

Stella smirks. "But you still got jealous."

"When he touched you, of course. But I knew you didn't want him, so that helped."

In synchronization, our heads turn just in time to see Juniper kiss her so-called date on the cheek. He just stands there, hands stuffed into his pockets, not bothering to pull her in close. And the way Juniper eyes him is not romantic, but conspiratorial.

There's also the fact that while they talk, he's checking out another woman across the bar.

Stella lifts a brow. "Should we tell him?"

Jasper shrugs. "We said we wouldn't get involved."

I drag my eyes away from Juniper for a moment. "Tell me what?"

Stella leans in. "That guy isn't Juniper's date. It's her friend, Wiley. They've known each other since they were in diapers."

Jasper scoffs. "We've known each other since we were eight and we're really together." He taps the diamond ring on her finger with a smug grin. "We're engaged now."

"Yeah, but Wiley and Juniper are different than you and me. We've always had chemistry."

Jasper smirks. "Glad you're willing to admit that."

Then, quieter, he reaches for her hand. "You're the only person I've ever looked at and known—absolutely known—I'd spend my life with."

She softens. "Good. Because you're stuck with me."

They share this look. So familiar, so full of ease and certainty, that it hits me square in the chest. The quiet kind of love. The kind that doesn't need proving. The kind that doesn't flinch when someone kisses the wrong cheek or pretends to care about someone else.

I look away.

Because I've never had that.

But I want it.

God help me, I want it with Juniper Jensen.

As Jasper and Stella get pulled into another conversation with local friends, I take the opportunity to reassess my approach, then head for the opposite end of the bar to grab a drink.

After settling with the bartender, I turn my attention back to Wiley and Juniper but as luck would have it, Juniper has left Wiley to talk to another friend on the other side of the bar.

As I approach, Wiley gulps back the rest of his beer just in time for me to set a fresh one in front of him.

He eyes it with interest before looking up at me.

"Liam Hargrove." I extend a hand, and he cautiously takes it. It's clear he knows who I am and the heartache I've caused his friend.

"Wiley Cooke."

"Brought you a fresh beer. Nutcracker Stout, right?"

"Yeah. How'd you know?" He glances around.

"I'm very observant."

He eyes my glass of whiskey.

"No offense, but you look like you drink cocktails I can't pronounce."

"Are you calling me pretentious, Wiley?"

"Um, not in a mean way." His eyes snag on my watch. "Just you're fancy and stuff."

"I appreciate what you're doing for her," I say.

"What do you mean?"

"Pretending you're on a date."

He smirks, but I catch the way his eyes flash with panic. Nervously, he picks up the beer I offered and takes a drink, his hand shaking when he returns it to the pub table. "W-we're not pretending."

"So, you let your date get her own drink?" I motion to Juniper at the bar with her friend.

"Maybe. And what exactly are you doing here?" he challenges.

"I'm here to prove something. To her—and to myself." I pause, gauging his reaction. "She might be pretending with you, but I'm not pretending with her."

Wiley crosses his arms, skeptical. "Nice watch. Bet it costs more than my car."

I glance at the watch face. I don't buy much for myself— never cared about cars or suits or flashy toys. But watches? They make sense to me. Precision. Craftsmanship. A promise that time, at least, can be measured and mastered. Which is more than I can say for the chaos in my chest every time Juniper looks at me like she hates me.

"I'm not here to play games. And I know you have another agenda for the night." I lift my brows, then nod my head toward the blonde across the room.

"Listen, man, Juni's not a fan of yours, so maybe you take the hint and move on."

"Can't. Not when I've spent a year wishing I could take back the moment I let her go."

He sighs, conflicted. "Shit, man, I can't compete with that."

"Don't worry. You don't have to."

"I know, but Juni asked me to—"

My brows lift at his near confession.

He sighs. "She's going to kill me."

I pat him on the shoulder. "You did good, Wiley. I'll deal with Juniper."

He looks thankful to be relieved from fake date duty and ready to start chatting up the blonde across the bar.

"But before you make your move, let's have a little fun."

"What kind of fun?" he asks, lifting the beer up to his lips.

Juniper, with drink in hand and a quick wave to the group of people she was talking to, heads our way.

The moment she spots me at the table with Wiley, her stride slows. Her eyes turn wary, like she's approaching a live grenade.

Wiley, looking far too pleased with himself, says, "Hey, Juni, we've got a problem."

She arches a brow. "We?"

I lean back on the barstool. "Wiley and I have reached an impasse."

She crosses her arms. "Oh, have you?"

"Yes," I say, sipping my drink. "We both seem to think we're your boyfriend."

She chokes on her drink. "Excuse me?"

Wiley, more committed to this bit than he was to being

her fake date, nods solemnly. "And it's getting messy, Juni. You need to clear this up."

"Traitor," she hisses at him.

I smirk. "So, which one of us gets the honor?"

She rolls her eyes. "Wiley, obviously."

Wiley raises a hand. "Ah, hold on—before you answer too fast, let's make it fair."

I gesture graciously. "Yes, let's give her the full picture."

Wiley straightens up. "Boyfriend Candidate #1: Me. I'd make a fine fake boyfriend. I don't ask too many questions, I have excellent taste in Christmas movies, and I don't—" He jerks a thumb at me, "—smirk like that."

I tilt my head. "Oh, I rather like my smirk."

I remember the moment last year at the liquor store when Juniper told me she liked it, too.

"Juni, I really like this guy." He takes a sip of the beer I bought him.

Juniper scowls. "Unbelievable."

I place a hand over my heart. "Which brings us to Boyfriend Candidate #2: Me. Not easily distracted, always listening, and..." I step closer, voice low, words just for her. "I wouldn't be faking it."

I hear the catch in her breath. She goes still.

"So, Juniper. Who's it going to be?"

Her eyes burn into mine. "Neither of you." She glares at Wiley. "I'll deal with you later."

"Good luck, man." Wiley hits me with a clap on the shoulder before heading in the direction of the blonde he's been eyeing.

Juniper is already pulling on her coat and heading for the door.

"Juniper! Wait!"

"Why can't you leave me alone?" she groans. "Is this

fun for you? Catching me in a lie and making me look silly?"

"Don't be mad at Wiley, I'm obnoxiously charming. He didn't stand a chance."

"You're something, that's for sure."

She yanks open the door and we're met with a blast of icy air.

As we pour out onto the sidewalk, snow is falling in large, heavy clumps. It'd be a magical night if not for the way Juniper is stomping off like she's trying to leave a trail of fury behind her.

"Juniper, slow down. I don't want you to get hurt."

She whirls around so fast she nearly collides with me. Her cheeks are flushed, eyes bright with emotion.

"Oh, that's rich coming from the man who humiliated me last year." Her voice is a sharp whisper, but it hits harder than if she'd shouted. "Don't worry, Liam. I'm a big girl. I can handle myself."

I bite my tongue, letting a group of patrons pass by and slip into the bar behind us.

"I never meant to hurt you," I say carefully. "But pretending nothing happened between us—acting like it didn't matter—that was a mistake."

"You don't get to rewrite the past just because you've decided you might feel something now."

Her voice cracks slightly, and I see the desperation in her eyes. She hates it.

She takes another step back and that's when her heel skids on a slick patch of snow.

## FIVE
## JUNIPER

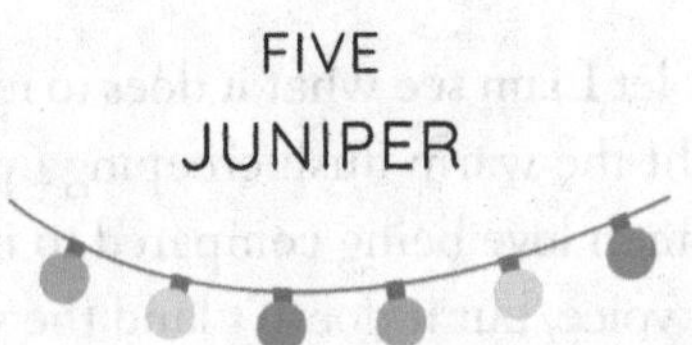

FOR THE SECOND TIME TODAY, Liam's words catch me off guard. The only thing my body knows to do with that is retreat.

Needing space, I take a step back but it's too quick, causing me to teeter backwards on the points of my stiletto heels.

Suddenly, I'm sliding. Falling backwards. My stomach drops in anticipation of feeling the cold, hard thud of the freshly snow-packed sidewalk underneath me, but it never comes. Liam's strong arms are my safety net.

"I got you, Firefly."

My head snaps up. *Firefly?*

I wrinkle my nose, but it's pure defense because something soft flares in my chest. I glance up to find relief etched into the features of his gorgeous face.

"Firefly?"

He shrugs, but there's something careful in the way he holds me. "You said June Bug felt too childish. I figured Firefly is the grown-up version."

It shouldn't get to me. But dammit, I love a good nickname, especially one that sounds like it means something. And this one from him? It feels like a secret. Like a promise. And how easily it rolled off his tongue? It's like he's thought about it for longer than the two seconds it took for him to catch me.

But I can't let Liam see what it does to me.

I try to fight the warm flush creeping up my neck. "You know how women love being compared to insects." I try for an edge to my voice, but it doesn't land the way I want it to, coming out more awestruck than angry.

He smiles, soft and steady. "I wasn't thinking of a bug. I was thinking of something small but impossible to ignore. Bright, unexpected. You walk into a room and everything changes a little. Like when fireflies show up, suddenly the night feels more magical."

My chest aches at how easily he says it, like it costs him nothing. Like it doesn't undo me.

Our warm breath mingles in the wintry air, filling the space between us with puffs of mist. Between the haze of our breathing, I can't stop myself from staring at his lips. From being mesmerized by the indented groove above his upper lip that gives his mouth fullness.

And the way it feels to be wrapped up in his arms? I'd stay here forever if I could.

Liam doesn't seem to mind our proximity, not like he did last year when he freaked out about our kiss. About me asking him to be my first.

*Don't be that desperate girl,* I remind myself before shrugging out of his embrace.

"Thanks." I clear my throat before proceeding to walk again.

This time, the smooth soles of my boots slide, then the stiletto heel follows with a skitter. If these stiletto boots were a problem before, they're even worse now that the snow has picked up. I stare down the icy, snow-covered path back toward my apartment. I'd wanted to impress Liam, to combat the embarrassment I felt last year, by wearing these sexy boots and now the only safe way home is to crawl. The irony isn't lost on me.

"You have a few options," Liam says from behind me. "Piggy-back or Fireman's carry?"

I whirl on him, staying focused on keeping my balance. "Excuse me?"

He shrugs, all smug in his perfectly weather-appropriate boots. "You know those boots won't make it another foot, let alone four blocks. So, which will it be?"

I lift my chin. "Neither. I'll just crawl. With dignity."

He chuckles under his breath. "Right. Very dignified."

"I'll be fine," I huff, though I'm already wobbling again as I try to take a step.

He raises an eyebrow. "Right. Totally convincing."

I stop, heel skidding slightly, and curse under my breath. I could insist on powering through, but I've nearly fallen twice, and pride isn't worth a broken ankle. I exhale sharply, then gingerly turn to face him again.

"Fine," I mutter. "But if you drop me, I swear to—"

He grins, stepping forward. "Piggy-back it is."

"Hey! I didn't say which one—"

"Too late. I've made an executive decision."

"Liam—"

"Up you go, Firefly."

He bends down and places his hands on the outside of my thighs, then lifts me up and onto his back. Instinctively, my arms wrap around his neck, pressing my front flush with his back.

I sigh, tightening my grip around his neck. Loving the

feel of being this close to him and hating myself for it at the same time.

"You good back there?" he asks.

I make a non-committal shrug, but to shield myself from the falling snow, I lower down closer to him. My head now tucked against the side of his, breathing in the scent of his cologne—balsam wood and pine with a hint of cinnamon. The urge to run my nose along the sliver of skin between his coat collar and the nape of his neck is strong.

I'm so distracted by all the Liam overload that I don't even realize we've made it the four blocks to the shelter of the awning that is shared by my store and my apartment entrance.

*Damn. I wish that walk was longer.*

*Click.*

The sound of a photo being taken catches me off guard.

"What was that?" I jolt slightly on his back. "Did you just take a picture?"

"You looked cute." He glances over his shoulder with a smug grin. "Couldn't resist."

"Delete it."

"Nope."

I wiggle, trying to slide down, but he hikes me higher and laughs.

"That one's going on my screensaver."

"You wouldn't."

I finally manage to slide off his back and reach for his phone, but he pulls it up and away.

"You're not keeping that. Give it to me!"

He grins wider, backing toward the door that leads to my apartment. "Not a chance. You're going to want it later."

The only reason I'd want it later is so I can print it out and draw devil horns on Liam's head.

"Yeah, I don't think so." I leap, trying to snatch his phone.

Thankfully, the wide awning above us has kept this patch of sidewalk clear of snow, giving me enough traction to jump and lunge like a woman on a mission.

What follows is probably ridiculous to anyone walking by: me jumping and lunging, him dodging and blocking with his free hand while laughing like a smug, aggravating man who knows he's got the upper hand.

"You haven't even seen the photo. It's really good."

Finally, I catch his wrist and tackle him against the doorframe—hard enough that the glass inset rattles and we're both breathless.

He grins down at me, our faces inches apart. "Careful, Firefly. You keep pinning me against walls, I might start getting ideas."

My cheeks flame at his teasing, but my task isn't complete, so I focus on twisting the phone from his grip and pull up the photo.

"Got it," I say, triumphant yet winded.

"Give it back," Liam says, tone low and smug behind me. "You're going to regret it."

I ignore him, thumb flying to the last image. And then, I freeze.

It's devastating. Annoyingly perfect. The snow swirling gently around us, my cheeks flushed, arms looped around his neck as I press close. I'm smiling—genuinely smiling—like I'm lost in thought but loving every minute of the ride. And Liam's grinning like I've always belonged there.

It's warm. Romantic. Aesthetically ideal. Like the kind of picture people put on engagement announcements and Pinterest vision boards.

I love it...but I don't want to.

Scowling, I hit delete. "Nope. Absolutely not."

Liam just smirks, totally unbothered.

"What?" I narrow my eyes.

He shrugs, casually brushing snow from his coat. "It's already backed up."

My mouth drops. "You didn't."

"Synced to the cloud. And messaged to myself." He shrugs, grinning. "That photo is a masterpiece. There was no way I was trusting your trigger-happy delete finger."

"You are such a—"

"Genius? Romantic? Devastatingly charming man?"

I shove the phone into his chest, trying to hide the fact that I'm flustered. And hating the fact that a simple photo is derailing all the progress I made moving past my feelings for Liam.

But it's not just the photo. He still hasn't said anything. No apology. No explanation. No declaration. Just maddeningly charming grins and a thousand mixed signals.

I don't like being played with, especially not by someone who already burned me once. If he wants something from me, he's going to have to use actual words. Otherwise, I'll keep my heart right where it is. Safe behind the wall I built after he rejected me last Christmas.

Stepping inside, I dust off the snow that's accumulated on my hat and coat before climbing the narrow, creaky stairs to my apartment.

Inside, the warmth hits immediately, and I'm thankful for my cozy sanctuary. But then Liam walks in behind me and all the stress returns. Dropping my stiletto boots on the drying mat, I start toward the kitchen. I need a buffer, a task. Anything.

Liam follows. I can feel him standing in the doorway, watching me.

"You know where the guest room is."

"I do."

I wait for him to leave, but he doesn't. I don't want to feel like this. Like I'm dying a little and there's nothing I can do about it.

"You know—" I start, turning to face him.

"I'll stay out of your way," he says, his voice quiet. "But if you think I came all this way just to sleep down the hall and pretend nothing happened between us, you don't know me very well."

My heart lurches. I move to brush past him, but he catches my wrist gently, barely a touch.

"I know you don't owe me anything," he murmurs. "Just don't shut me out completely. Please."

I look up at him, startled by the rawness in his voice.

My defenses crack for half a second, and that's all it takes. Our eyes lock and I know he must see right through me because the air between us goes thick.

"Goodnight," I say, my voice not nearly as firm as I want it to be.

Liam releases me, nods once, then disappears down the hallway.

When I hear the door to the guest bedroom shut, I allow myself to drop onto a chair at my small kitchen table.

It's been mere hours with Liam, and I already feel myself sinking back into old feelings. I just need to make it to Christmas.

SIX

LIAM

I TAP my phone on the payment screen and smile when the photo of me and Juniper from last night lights up. I wasn't kidding when I told her I was going to make it my screensaver.

I'd woken up early. Juniper's guest bed was comfortable, yet with my brain being on eastern time, I couldn't sleep past five thirty. So instead, I answered some emails, then ten minutes ago, walked down the street to The Hollow Bean to grab us chocolate croissants and coffees. I'd become obsessed with the croissants during my short visit to Cedar Hollow last year. Little did I know they wouldn't be my only obsession with this town.

The sidewalks lining Founders Street are shoveled and now cleared of ice, but last night the slick sidewalks paired with sexy stiletto boots that had no place in a Colorado snowstorm had been the catalyst for getting close to Juniper.

She'd begrudged the piggy-back ride but then I'd caught the look on her face in the photo I'd taken, and it gave me hope.

I glance down at the screensaver on my phone again.

Juniper's eyes are on me, with an unmistakable softness to them. Her mouth curved into a wistful, almost vulnerable expression, like she's savoring something she doesn't think she can have.

But she has me. She just doesn't know it yet.

I want her. I've wanted her since that night. But wanting someone and being ready for them are two different things—and last year, I wasn't. I panicked. I messed up.

But rushing into some grand apology or kissing her the second I got here wouldn't fix anything. It might make me feel better, but it wouldn't make her trust me again. And I want her trust. Her belief that I mean what I say. That this isn't just guilt or nostalgia or lust. It's more.

Now, I'm not just trying to win her back. I'm trying to show her that she's not a passing infatuation. I see a future with her.

So yeah, for now I'm holding back. Not because I'm unsure, but because I'm sure and I don't want to mess it up again.

Grabbing the pastry bag and tray of coffees in one hand, I exit the café.

On my way back to Juniper's flat, I pass by the storefront under construction. The soon-to-be wine bar currently with brown butcher's paper covering the windows.

Glancing around, I note that the newly plowed streets are empty and outside of the few people making a similar run to the café, most of Cedar Hollow is still asleep.

I set the pastry bag and coffees down, then reach for the lock box. Putting in the code releases the back, and a single key falls out.

Once I'm inside the space, the scent of freshly sanded

oak mingles with plaster dust and paint. My boots echo faintly against the unfinished wood floor.

The pictures my project manager, Ellen, sent me don't do it justice.

The drywall's up. The custom shelves are in, still bare, but the bones are solid. The bar counter—dark walnut with a matte finish—is finally installed, and even under the protective covering, it looks like something out of a magazine. Clean lines, rich wood, subtle character.

Tools are scattered, painter's tape still clings to baseboards, and there's a bucket sitting in the middle of the floor collecting a slow drip from an unfinished pipe. It's a mess, but it's *my* mess. And it's starting to look like the real thing.

A local artist just finished the mural on the far wall. It's a delicate line drawing of intertwined grapevines, curling and climbing like they're growing up toward the ceiling.

I walk the length of the space, trailing a hand over the wall where the built-in wine racks will go. In the back corner chairs in plastic wrap are stacked up. I can picture the layout clearly now. It's intimate and a little moody, but nothing too trendy. Just *timeless*.

One of the pendant lights swings slightly overhead, catching my eye. I'd gone with soft brass for the hardware; against the deep green paint I'd second-guessed for a week until I'd asked *JuniReads* her opinion in the county's small-business forum chat. Now, seeing it all together under the dim construction lights, I know. She was right.

I exhale slowly. This place is coming together. It's not ready for the soft opening yet, and I still have a hundred things to figure out. But for the first time since I started this project, I feel it. *This is going to work.*

My phone buzzes with a text from Beck, my younger

brother. He's twenty-four, and currently on holiday with some friends at a ski resort.

BECK

How's the whole "redeeming yourself with Juniper" mission going?

I groan, already knowing exactly where this is going.

Fine. Everything is under control.

BECK

You can't just tiptoe around like a scared accountant and expect a happy ending.

Thanks for the pep talk. Really needed that.

BECK

Always happy to lecture my brilliant older brother.

And you're giving me tips because…?

BECK

I'm charming and decisive. I've got a knack for handling these types of situations. Also, because someone has to make sure you don't screw this up again. But mostly, I like to watch you squirm.

You're terrible.

BECK

Terrible? Me? Never. Look, if you need an intervention, or a wingman, I'm just a phone call away.

I sigh, tucking my phone back in my pocket, shaking my head at how he always finds a way to get under my skin.

Beck has a way of making even the most serious moments feel ridiculous—and somehow, it keeps me grounded.

Beck and Jasper, along with my parents, are the few that know about the wine bar and the reason I'm laying down roots in Cedar Hollow.

Creating a business next door to Juniper's—while she still carries a healthy dose of dislike for me—might seem insane to anyone else. Jasper calls it madness. I call it opportunity. The definition of insanity is doing the same thing over and over and expecting different results, right? Well, this is my calculated kind of insane. Never in my life have I pursued a woman the way I plan to pursue Juniper. All in. No holding back. So much skin in the game that I could get burned.

And yet, I wouldn't have it any other way.

I take a few photos then send them to Ellen with notes before locking up and heading back to Juniper's flat.

Like her romance bookstore, Juniper's flat radiates warmth and whimsy. Simply being in her space puts me at ease.

When I set the bag of pastries on the wooden coffee table, I notice a stack of books.

The one on top has different colored tabs sticking out of the pages. I pick it up and flip through it. In addition to the tabs, some of the text is highlighted. There are hearts and other doodles next to passages, some even have notes written out.

*Would not say no.*

*Why don't real men talk like this?*

*Mirror scenes will always win. Top-tier filth. 10/10 would reread (and reenact).*

The creaky wooden floors announce Juniper's arrival, so

I set the book back on the coffee table and grab the bag of pastries.

"Morning."

She's in a corduroy skirt with thick patterned tights on beneath, an oversized cardigan with heart buttons and a t-shirt underneath that says, *"Reading Is My Love Language."*

"I got you a coffee and a chocolate croissant."

She studies me a beat before taking the outreached bag and coffee. When she leans in, I catch her signature scent, warm plum and vanilla.

"Thank you, but you didn't have to do that."

"I wanted to."

She nods, like she's not quite sure what to say.

"What are your plans today?"

"Probably hang out here." I glance around her cozy living room, my eyes landing on that gingerbread advent calendar with the tiny painted doors all lined up in perfect rows. "Look through your stuff."

Her polite smile falters. *"Excuse me?"*

I grin. "Kidding. I've got a few meetings."

She crosses her arms, one eyebrow arching as she leans against the bookshelf like she's settling in for a standoff. "Couldn't you do that from...I don't know...literally anywhere else? Like your shiny corner office?"

I shrug, taking a sip of my coffee. "Could've."

She tilts her head, studying me like she's trying to solve a puzzle I haven't given her all the pieces for. "So...what is this, Liam? A working vacation? Business trip? Or you just like Cedar Hollow's stunning December weather?"

"Something like that." I keep my tone light, but her eyes narrow at my deflection.

We're standing too close. The quiet hum of her flat

makes the air feel thick. She's staring at my mouth like she wants to say something—do something—reckless.

I take a step closer, dropping my voice just enough to make her shiver. "Maybe I like the view better here."

Her breath catches. I see it—the spark, the wanting—before she shuts it down with a tight shake of her head. She backs up a step, clutching her coffee cup like it might save her.

"I don't have time for this," she says, more to herself than me. "I have things to—"

I smirk, savoring the way her words run together when I get too close. "Relax, Firefly. I'll get out of your hair."

She scowls at the nickname but doesn't fight me on it this time.

I tap the lid of my coffee, then brush past her—close enough that my arm grazes her side.

"I'm going to take a shower. Try not to miss me too much while I'm gone."

She lets out a sound between a laugh and a scoff but doesn't answer. She's too busy glaring at my back as I disappear down the hallway.

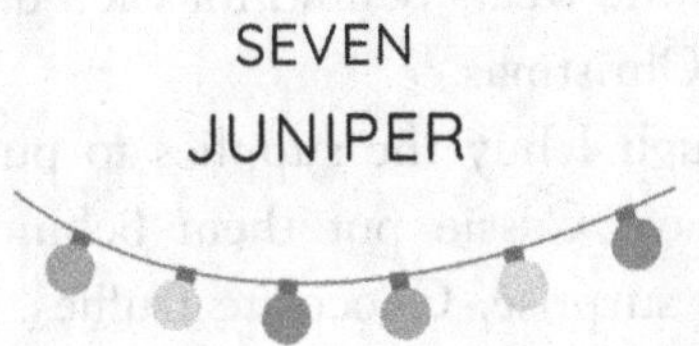

I WAIT for Liam to disappear down the hallway before I pop in my ear buds and hit play on my audiobook. It's how I spend my mornings. Listening to a book while I eat breakfast and plan out the day's tasks.

With the Books & Bubbly event this coming weekend, I need to get the shelves restocked by the end of the week so the store will be ready. There are at least twenty new boxes of books that need to be put out. Charlotte, my assistant at the store, has been a huge help with keeping everything organized.

I take another bite of croissant, ignoring the warmth that spreads through my chest at the thought of Liam knowing they are my favorite. While I jot down a few notes, I listen to the start of a tension-filled scene between Micheala and her ex's older brother, Johnathan. Knowing this scene is going to be so good I should annotate it, I jump up to grab the paperback from the living room.

On my way there, I'm licking the chocolate off my lips when I pass my advent calendar and stop in front of it.

I used to make paper chains with the number of links to

represent how many days there were until Christmas. I loved the satisfaction of watching the chain shrink each day when I tore the paper to remove a link. The equivalent now is my DIY gingerbread house advent calendar with doors that I've put little treats behind for each day of December leading up to Christmas.

Even though I buy the supplies to put in the advent calendar, I have Cassie put them behind each door so they're still a surprise. Chocolate truffles, my favorite lip balm, trial size beauty products, and cute bookish items like stickers and keychains.

Opening the door each day is the first thing I do after I get ready, but Liam being here had distracted me. I mean when doesn't that man distract me?

Sleeping last night had been no exception.

Knowing Liam was on the other side of my bedroom wall didn't help.

Every creak of the floorboards, every muffled shift of blankets, it all kept me wide awake and way too aware that the man who once kissed me like I was something fragile and dangerous was now only one thin wall away.

At one point, I'd rolled over, punched my pillow, and told myself to *stop thinking about him.* Which of course made me think about him more. Like how broad his shoulders looked in my tiny hallway, or the smug grin he wears when he knows he's under my skin.

*Focus.*

I hit pause on my earbud to stop the playback, then reach for the bright pink door numbered eighteen.

Inside is my favorite lip balm, raspberry cloud, in the limited-edition holiday packaging. Again, it's not a surprise but there's still a rush of satisfaction to see what is inside each day. I grab the lip balm, but my fingers brush against something else tucked behind it.

Reaching in farther, I pull out a silk hairbow in a soft blush color.

I do love a good hairbow and pink is my favorite color, but I don't recall buying this one.

It's dainty. Pretty. I glance down—and would go perfectly with my outfit today.

I'm heading for the bathroom mirror to try it out all while curiosity has me wondering where it came from.

Maybe Cassie snuck it in.

Or my mom?

In the bathroom, a thin veil of steam hangs in the air from Liam's recent shower. Using the mirror to guide me, I pull half of my hair back and wrap the hairbow around it.

Glancing in the mirror, I turn my head side to side to admire the way the soft pink bow complements my dark red hair. It's sweet. It's feminine. It's—

"Pretty."

I nearly jump out of my skin at the sound of Liam's voice.

When I turn, I find him standing in the doorway, freshly showered, a towel wrapped low on his hips.

My breath catches, and I try not to look, but fail.

Water clings to the edge of his jaw. And his perfectly golden bare chest.

Damn. This is not very helpful to my morning routine. Or my sanity.

His entire chest is on display, and it's unfair how devastating he looks.

My eyes zero in on his tattoos. The one beneath his collar bone. The one across his ribs. And the one on the inside of his right arm. The tattoos he revealed with every holiday drink sample we consumed. Then there are the ones I haven't seen. Another handful in various places that have my eyes feasting with each new discovery.

"Did you need something?" I ask, eyes now firmly fixed on my own reflection.

He doesn't move. Just leans one shoulder against the doorframe, his gaze flicking up to the ribbon in my hair.

"Just admiring the view."

I give him a look.

"The bow," he clarifies, smile tugging at his mouth. "You always looked good in pink."

For a moment, it feels like we're back to that flirty, chemistry-laced place we were last year at the liquor store. When I thought I felt something bubbling between us. Something warm, real, and maybe even worth hoping for.

How wrong I'd been.

I'm not about to mistake kindness for intention. Not again.

"Like you noticed," I mutter.

"What was that?"

"I'm not wearing it for you," I say, loud and deliberately.

"Didn't say you were." His dark eyes spark with amusement, all smug and utterly Liam. "But that doesn't mean I don't appreciate it."

He pushes off the doorframe, stepping past me to the second sink at the vanity.

As he passes by, I inhale a familiar scent.

Winter plum. It's the scent of my seasonal shampoo.

"Did you use my shampoo?" I ask.

"Yeah, I forgot to pack some. Hope that's okay?" His smile widens, picking up the razor on the counter. "It smells good. Festive."

My mouth opens, but nothing comes out because now

all I'm picturing is Liam standing in my shower, steam curling around him, water running down his chest, descending his stomach to where his—

I stop my runaway thoughts, refusing to think about Liam's naked body in the shower. Imagining what it would be like if had his hand wrapped around his—damn it, I just did it again.

Gah. I need to get control of this situation.

"I guess if you want to smell like a girl," I tease.

"Not just a girl." He dips his razor under the faucet, his eyes meeting mine in the mirror. "Like you."

That shouldn't sound provocative. It shouldn't make heat unfurl low in my stomach like a match has been struck, but it does.

"You know, I might've used that purple loofah, too. The fluffy one hanging on the hook."

The razor slides against his jaw. He looks so casual, shaving in my bathroom like he's done it a thousand times, and he plans to do it another thousand more.

It's fascinating and sexy, and I hate that I can't stop staring at him. Can't stop wondering what it would be like if he were here every morning.

"W-what exactly did you do with it?" I cross my arms, trying not to squirm.

He dips the razor back under the faucet, then tilts his head like he's pretending to think it over. "I don't know. What do you usually do with it?"

My eyes narrow. "That's none of your business."

He finishes his shave, then grabs a hand towel to pat his smooth jaw dry while I continue to openly stare at him.

Still looking too comfortable with one of my bath towels wrapped around his trim waist, he turns in my direction.

"Did you need something, Firefly?" he asks, teasingly throwing my words back at me.

"Yes." I swallow hard, but force myself to take what I hope to be an intimidating step toward him, my jaw tightening at how irritated, yet turned on, I am. "My apartment back."

Liam doesn't flinch. He just smirks, cool and confident. "Your flat?" he repeats, his grin turning lazy. "I'm not here for the real estate, Juniper. I came for what I left behind."

My mind races with what he could be referring to.

Reading my confusion, he edges closer. I get a whiff of winter plum a la Liam. It's my scent, but on him, it's something else. The holidays wrapped in sin and spice.

"You."

THE DOOR SLAMS shut with more force than necessary.

Progress.

Not that leaving a woman flustered and calling it a win is typical for me. But Juniper Jensen isn't just any woman. She's *the one*. And she's determined to box me up as an old mistake she's outgrown. Like I'm just her embarrassing crush she's buried under shiny new dreams.

She has no idea I didn't come here to sleep under her roof and tiptoe around old feelings. I came to reveal they were never one-sided like she thinks.

I flip open my laptop at her kitchen table, her scent still clinging to the sweater she left draped on the back of the chair. There's already a message waiting in the Summit County Small-Business forum.

*JuniReads: Hey! Just confirming the prosecco delivery for the Books & Bubbly event this weekend? And any chance you have an extra case? Demand's higher than I guessed.*

When she opened Blush & Binding, I'd wanted to help. I'd wanted to keep some piece of her life connected to mine without crossing any lines. *PourChoices* was supposed to be a one-time favor. An anonymous screen name on the Summit County Small-Business forum. Free business advice. A few marketing suggestions. A distraction for me to stop replaying the look on her face when I turned her down last Christmas.

But then she kept writing back.

And I couldn't help myself.

Now she trusts *PourChoices* more than she trusts me, the real me. She tells him things she'd never say to my face. She lets him see her worries, her excitement, the dreams she won't admit out loud. It's like a second chance, without her knowing I'm the man she's talking to.

Maybe that makes me an asshole. Maybe it's the only way to fix what I broke. Either way, I'm not letting it go. Not yet.

*PourChoices: An extra case is no problem.*

*JuniReads: I'll repay you in chocolate croissants from The Hollow Bean. That is, once you finally reveal yourself.*

I grin at her sweet bribe and start typing.

*PourChoices: Careful—pastries are my weakness. I might end up agreeing to more than just wine deliveries.*

Her typing bubble pops up immediately.

*JuniReads: Dangerous knowledge to give me. I didn't sleep well last night, so I might bribe you for more than wine.*

A pulse of satisfaction runs through me. No sleep? Wonder why.

*PourChoices: Not second-guessing the event, are you? You've thought of everything. It'll be brilliant.*

*JuniReads: Nope. The event is fine. It's my surprise holiday house guest that's the problem.*

I bite back a laugh.

*PourChoices: I thought you liked surprises?*

*JuniReads: Not this one. It's very annoying. Tall. Smug.*

*Way too good at smirking. And apparently thinks my apartment is a hotel.*

My grin turns downright feral.

*PourChoices: Sounds like trouble. Should I sneak you a bottle early for stress relief?*

*JuniReads: You going to delivery it personally? Or are you too mysterious for that?*

I lean back in my chair, imagining her at her desk in the bookstore office below me, typing this out in that fuzzy sweater she wore this morning. That pink bow making her look like a present I want to unwrap.

*PourChoices: Unfortunately, I won't be able to deliver in person. I haven't been able to make the move yet, but I'm getting closer.*

She sends back a suspicious emoji.

*JuniReads: You have an occupancy date yet?*

*PourChoices: Not yet, but things are coming together nicely. Should be soon.*

*JuniReads: I can't wait to see it. Would be nice to have a distraction from the chaos of my unplanned roommate.*

I can feel her frustration through the screen.

*PourChoices: Hang in there. Take ten minutes in that reading nook of yours.*

The second I hit send; I curse under my breath. Shit. Too specific.

Her reply comes fast.

*JuniReads: How do you know I have a reading nook?*

I stare at her words for a beat, fighting the urge to laugh at my own slip. Being around her again has made me careless.

I crack my knuckles and type.

*PourChoices: Doesn't every cozy independent bookstore have one?*

A pause. Then her typing bubble pops up again.

*JuniReads: You're right. They should.*

I blow out a breath, leaning back in my chair. The quiet creaks of the old building remind me she's just below me. Close enough that if I wanted to, I could find her in seconds.

But I've got work to do. And not just the kind I can hide behind a screen for.

I STARE at the message blinking back at me: *Hang in there. Take ten minutes in that reading nook of yours.*

I blink once. Twice.

Did I ever tell *PourChoices* I have a reading nook? I don't think so.

Sure, lots of indie bookstores have them. But mine isn't exactly obvious. It's tucked behind the table display of tropes and staff picks, between the stacks on the north side of the store, opposite the wall with built-in shelves and ladder. A battered blush velvet chair, a basket of knit blankets in every shade of pink and cream, a little side table I found at a vintage market last spring.

It's not official. It's *mine*. My soft landing when the chaos gets too loud. Where I hide with an annotated paperback and a mug of something sweet when the weight of keeping this dream alive feels heavier than I can hold.

I scroll up through my old messages with *PourChoices*, just to be sure. Did I mention it when we talked about his wine bar opening next door? When we swapped marketing ideas? Nope. Nothing.

A prickle of suspicion dances down my neck, but my phone buzzes on the counter.

It's Charlotte.

CHARLOTTE

Hey Juni, I hate to do this, but I can't make my shift today. Oliver's running a fever, and I can't find anyone to watch him.

Perfect. Absolutely perfect.

I let out a groan that echoes off the walls of shelves. No help during the biggest holiday rush of the year. It'll be just me, my peppermint latte that's gone cold, and a line of romance lovers needing recommendations, gift wrap, and for me to remember where I put the new shipment of special editions.

I glance back at my laptop. The chat with *PourChoices* is still open.

Part of me wants to type back: *How do you know about the nook?*

But my thumb freezes. There's no time. There's no headspace for that mystery today.

So I shove my phone into my skirt pocket, straighten my new *Come for the Tropes, Stay for the Spice* sign by the register, and force a smile for the first customer of the day.

Questions can wait. *PourChoices* can wait. Liam can definitely wait.

Right now, the only thing that can't wait is my bookstore.

It's early afternoon when three women approach the

counter with their purchases. A mother and her two daughters similar in age to me.

"This is the cutest store," one of the daughters gushes.

"Thank you." I grab a tote bag and start ringing up their books.

The mom makes a waving motion. "And he's a nice touch."

"I'm sorry. Who?" My brows dip as I scan another book.

"The gorgeous man who looks like a book boyfriend reading between the stacks." She cups her hand like she's sharing a secret. "His British accent is on point."

"It's like that account for hot dudes reading," one of the daughters notes. "You know, where people anonymously post hot guys reading in the wild?"

A man with a British accent reading in my store...what are the odds? Something tells me Liam would know.

*I'm going to kill him.*

I smile, but it's thin and murderous. "It's fake."

The mom blinks. "Wait—really?"

"Tragically American."

I force a polite smile, but under the surface, I'm already imagining Liam being shelved—face-first—into the mafia romance section.

After I ring them and another customer up, I make a beeline for the cozy reading nook between romantasy and LGBTQIA+ romance. There, in my carefully curated nook, I find Liam sprawled in the plush pink armchair like he pays rent here. Dark wool coat draped over the chair. Henley sleeves pushed up just enough to show an erotic amount of inked forearm. One ankle crossed over his knee like he's too cool to sit properly.

And in his hands? My annotated copy of Pippa Monroe's latest book.

My tabs. My notes. My secret desires.

"I'm sorry, is this your villain origin story?" I ask.

He barely glances up. "It might be. Chapter thirteen is particularly engrossing."

"Hey," I reach for the book, but he shifts back, holding it just out of reach. "You stole that from my apartment."

He shrugs, not fazed by my accusation. "Your coffee table is basically public domain."

His outstretched arm lifts his shirt, exposing a taunting sliver of hard abs. Of course.

"Yeah, well, that book is off limits."

I do my best not to ogle the unfair display, bracing my hands on the back of the chair as I lean closer, fingers stretching for the book.

With a smirk that's lazy and infuriating, he shifts it just out of reach.

It's just like last night with his phone and that photo he took of us.

He may have saved that photo in time, but this—my annotated book—he can't have.

I lunge a little harder, but it's a big mistake. My balance slips, the chair legs screech, and the next thing I know, I'm toppling straight into his lap with an ungraceful *oof*.

His free arm comes around my waist, steadying me like this was his plan all along.

"Chapter thirteen has a lot of tabs," he murmurs, voice warm against my ear. "I'm taking notes."

"Notes for what?" I snap, trying to twist away but only managing to settle in deeper against him.

"What you like."

Heat coils low in my belly, no matter how hard I glare.

"I'm this close to throwing you out."

"You won't." His grin widens and it's pure sin. "You're too intrigued by what I've learned."

He taps one of the pretty pink tabs with maddening precision. "You're a sucker for enemies-to-lovers. Slow burn. Banter. Forbidden tension. And apparently—" his eyes flick to mine, dark and wicked, "mirror sex."

My entire body bursts into flames. It's hard to pinpoint if I'm seething mad or turned on. Maybe both. It's our conversation in the bathroom this morning all over again.

"Those are fictional preferences," I hiss.

He shuts the book with a soft thud, his mouth so close I feel the brush of every word. "Then let's do a case study. Compare fantasy with reality. It'd be purely academic, of course."

"You're impossible."

"Just passionate." He winks. "And according to page 297, you like that."

I want to scream. Or kiss him. Or maybe throttle him.

Before I can decide which, I glance toward the checkout counter and freeze.

A line. A full-on holiday rush, half-off-bookmarks kind of line.

"Oh no."

Liam leans just enough to peek around me, his hand still warm on my waist. "Looks like your book boyfriend's popularity is contagious."

"I hate you." The dull ache between my legs says otherwise.

"You don't."

I shove at his chest, wriggling free of his lap in the least graceful escape imaginable. My knee bumps his thigh, he grins, quietly smug, and I shoot him a withering glare before I all but sprint for the register. The three customers in line are already starting to glance at their watches. I plaster on a customer-service smile like it's been stapled to my face and hop behind the counter, pointedly ignoring the heat still buzzing under my skin.

"Sorry about the wait! I—uh—was handling a plot twist." I reach for the book of the first customer. "You know how those go."

She smiles and nods. "Totally."

"I thought it was a mirror in chapter thirteen," Liam says casually as he strolls up beside me, like he belongs there. Like this is his store.

Just like my apartment this morning. He's got some nerve.

"You are not on the clock," I hiss under my breath as I scan the book.

"Then I'll consider this a volunteer position. Civic duty. Holiday spirit."

"*Liam.*"

But he's already turning to the customer. "Wasn't that just the cutest cover? I'm reading that one now—highly recommend. Dual POV, forced proximity, emotionally constipated hero. You'll love it."

The customer beams. "That's exactly what I was hoping for!"

Traitor.

Liam slips behind the counter next to me, and before I can stop him, he's ringing up a tote bag and chatting with the next person in line like he's done this his whole life. His sleeves are still pushed up, his forearm tattoos winking at me. And the stack of romance bookmarks he's handing out might as well be little green flags waving, *I read romance novels, give piggy-back rides, and I'll rub your feet.*

The piggy-back ride was nice, but there's no way I'm

letting him near my feet. Liam's thumbs digging into my arches while I suppress a guttural moan? I'd never recover.

I glance at him sideways, begrudgingly impressed.

"Where did you even learn how to do this?"

He shrugs. "I pay attention."

"You're a menace."

"I'm a multitasker."

Liam ends up helping me through the entire customer rush, somehow managing to charm every person while also upselling tote bags like it's his personal mission. I don't know if I'm impressed or horrified.

"You know, most people panic in retail chaos," I mutter as I bag up an entire stack of holiday romances.

"I thrive under pressure," he says, sliding a credit card back to a customer with a wink. "And I've got fast hands."

I've fantasized far too many times about the capabilities of Liam's hands, and it has gotten me nowhere.

"Stop talking."

A moment later, the bell above the door jingles again as the last customer leaves, and I finally exhale.

Liam glances around like he's soaking in every corner of my store before his eyes land back on me. "Looks like you figured it all out."

I think he's referring to my meltdown about the budget and marketing plan last Christmas, the one he was patiently helping me untangle before I decided to ruin everything by kissing him like a desperate idiot.

Part of me wants to let him think I did all this on my own. That I'm thriving and fully capable without his help. But I can't quite take all the credit.

I turn away and start organizing the bookish sticker carousel, most of which are holiday themed.

*Sleigh my TBR.*

*Merry and Bookish.*

*Hot Cocoa & Plot Twists.*

"I didn't do it alone," I admit.

"No?" Liam shifts, leaning one elbow on the counter beside me.

"There's this small-business forum for Summit County. One of the guys on there talks me through stuff sometimes. PourChoices—that's his username." I add, "P-O-U-R. Like pouring wine or whiskey. I don't actually know his real name."

Liam's quiet, but there's a telltale glint in his eyes. I'm suddenly babbling to fill the silence. "He's really smart. He helped me figure out my budget, and he listens to me rant about tropes. He's kind of the real deal."

"Hmm." He watches me with an unreadable expression. "Sounds like you're a fan."

I squint at him. "Why are you looking at me like that?"

"Nothing. Just wondering..." His mouth curves into a maddeningly smug grin. "Do you like him? More than a friend?"

"What? *No.*" I scoff, maybe too loudly. "First of all, I don't even know him. Second, what are you talking about?"

"First, Wiley. Now this forum guy. I'm starting to think I've got competition." He playfully arches a brow, but the fierce glint in his eyes gives him away. Just like last night, my body reacts to his overt jealousy by lighting up from the inside out.

I cross my arms to cover my quickly hardening nipples. "I'm not a complete weirdo who has a crush on a guy I've never met, Liam."

His grin grows, but his eyes soften with sincerity. "Good."

I glare, but it's not as sharp as I wish it was. The way

he's looking at me is making it harder to be annoyed with him.

"You got it from here?"

"Of course I do, it's my store."

He hovers closer, like he wants to say something. To do something. But I clear my throat, and he leans back.

"I'll see you later."

"Byeee!" I call to his retreating frame.

# TEN
## LIAM

AFTER SPENDING the afternoon at Juniper's bookstore, I know I should give her space. Be a courteous houseguest. Shut myself in the guest room and let her have her nightly routine without me in the way. But that's the thing: I don't want to be out of her way. I want to be right here. In the soft glow of her living room, warm lamplight spilling across her dog-eared books and half-finished mugs of tea.

She's in the kitchen, earbuds in and humming along to the holiday playlist she loves. She thinks she hums quietly— she doesn't. She sings "Last Christmas" loud and off-key. It's perfect.

"Jesus, Liam!" she screams, her mug of hot cocoa splashing everywhere. "Fuck!"

"Shit, Firefly. I'm sorry."

"What the hell are you thinking sneaking up on me?"

"I wasn't sneaking. I was waiting for you to finish your solo." I grin at how passionate her singing had been a moment ago.

"Don't grin at me like that," she snaps, cradling her

hand, cocoa dripping down her wrist. Her eyes shine with embarrassment and pain. "God, that's hot. Ow, ow, ow."

"Let me see." I reach for her, but she tries to twist away, glaring at me over her shoulder.

"I'm fine—"

"Juniper." My voice leaves no room for debate. I catch her wrist gently, turning it over to inspect the reddened skin. "Where's your first aid kit?"

She mutters something under her breath about bossy CFOs and points her chin toward the bathroom. I guide her to the couch instead. "Sit. I'll get it."

When I come back, she's perched at the edge of the cushion, fussing with the sleeves of her cardigan like she's trying to hide inside it. I kneel in front of her, first aid kit open at my side.

"It's not that bad," she protests as I dab at her skin with a cool cloth. She hisses and glares at me like it's my fault.

"It's okay to let someone take care of you."

Her eyes dart to mine. There's so much she wants to argue with in that sentence, I can see it. But the words never come out. She just watches me work, her lips pressed together.

When I'm done, I blow gently on the tender spot, half to soothe it, half because I can't resist. Her breath catches.

"There," I say, my voice lower now. "Good as new."

"Don't push it," she murmurs, but her tone is softer than before.

I ease back, giving her space she doesn't actually ask for. My gaze lands on the pile of half-wrapped books stacked on the coffee table.

"What are those?"

"The blind date with a book bingo prizes for my event this weekend."

"You can't finish these one-handed," I say. "You'll make a mess."

She snorts. "Oh, and you're a wrapping paper expert now?"

I raise an eyebrow. "Do you want help or not?"

She gives a dramatic sigh. "Fine. But if you ruin my aesthetic, I'm making you redo every single one."

"Deal." I sit beside her, our shoulders almost brushing. "What's the theme?"

She hands me a book, our fingers brushing. "The theme is *magic under the mistletoe*. Figure it out, genius."

I grin and reach for the tape. "You know, these hands are pretty capable. I think I can manage some tape and paper."

She rolls her eyes, but there's a ghost of a smile on her lips now. "We'll see."

She hits play on the TV. *While You Were Sleeping* flickers to life—Sandra Bullock in a bulky sweater, Chicago blanketed in snow.

Perfect.

We work in silence for a while—except for the movie dialogue and her occasional muttering when I fold a corner crooked. She keeps bossing me around like I'm a new hire at her little indie empire.

"Less tape, Hargrove," she says, pointing with her good hand. "Neater edges."

"Bossy," I mutter back. "You'd be a terrible subordinate."

Her eyes light with a wicked gleam. "Good thing I'm in charge."

She reaches to grab another book, but a small velvet box tumbles out from under a stack on the coffee table. I catch it before it hits the floor.

"What's this?" I ask, turning it over in my palm.

She freezes. Her eyes dart from the box to my face. "That's—That's nothing. Put it back."

I flip it open anyway. Inside is a vintage watch. Sleek. Timeless. Exactly my taste.

"Juniper." My chest tightens. "You were thinking about me," I say before I can stop myself.

Juniper's eyes go wide for a half-second before her spine stiffens. "Don't flatter yourself, Hargrove." She snatches the box from my hand, tucking it against her chest like she's protecting something fragile. "I got that months ago when I was furniture hunting. It was meant for Jasper to give to his best friend for Christmas. Congratulations. You just ruined your own surprise."

She lifts her chin, all defensive bravado and that sharp-edged pride I know too well.

I don't push it. I don't call her bluff, even if it's written all over her flushed cheeks and the way she won't quite meet my eyes.

I just nod, pretending to buy it. "Right. Then I'll act surprised."

"Yeah. Forget you saw it."

"Hard to forget something perfect," I say, but she's already tucking it behind a pillow, like it never existed.

She hits play again, trying to bury herself in the movie. I grab another book to wrap and lean close enough that our knees brush.

On screen, Sandra Bullock is telling Bill Pullman she's in love. Juniper's hair brushes my arm when she shifts, her lips parting around a smile when I mutter about the world's most crooked bow.

She sighs dramatically when I tape another bow lopsided.

"You're hopeless," she says, exasperated but soft. She shifts closer on the couch, tucking one leg under her. "Give me that."

She reaches for the half-wrapped book in my hands. Our fingers brush. Warm skin against warm skin. It sends a jolt up my arm that I swear she feels, too, judging by the way her breath hitches.

"Look—" She wrestles the crumpled ribbon from my fist, her thigh pressing against mine. "You have to loop it under first. Like this."

I lean closer, pretending I can't figure it out just to watch her work. Even with the burn on her hand, her fingers move with quick confidence, tugging the ribbon snug around the paper.

"Then twist here, hold with your thumb—" She grabs my hand, positioning my thumb exactly where she wants it. I'm not even watching the ribbon anymore. I'm watching her mouth, the way her teeth catch her lower lip when she concentrates.

"And pull this loop through..." She finishes the bow, tight and perfect.

When she looks up, she realizes how close we are, but neither of us moves right away. Our hands stay tangled in the ribbon, hers warm over mine.

"There." Her voice comes out softer than before. "It's perfect."

"Not bad," I murmur, but my eyes aren't on the bow. They're on her. She knows it, too. Her throat bobs in a swallow, her breath puffing out just a little too quick.

"Next one's yours," she says, forcing her hands away like she needs distance to breathe. "Try not to butcher it."

I pick up the next book, my fingers still tingling from where hers touched mine. "No promises."

# ELEVEN
## JUNIPER

IT'S BARELY 10:00 a.m. and I'm irritated.

Not at Charlotte, who is back at work after her son's fever broke last night, humming along to the instrumental holiday playlist as she straightens displays with far more care than necessary. Not at the new shipment of books stacked in the back room like a paper fortress waiting to topple. Not even at the coffee I spilled on my sweater earlier.

No, I'm annoyed because I haven't seen Liam all morning.

Which is ridiculous. That is the goal. Fewer run-ins with Liam are preferable. Right?

Because it's not like I need to see him. It's not like I'm waiting to see him.

It's not like I've been casually glancing toward the door every time I hear the bell jingle—because that would mean I care. And I don't.

I should be focused on the fact that my hot cocoa burn is puffy and tender, which makes shelving and typing and practically everything I do ache. That should be my biggest concern.

I shouldn't be thinking about Liam's first aid skills. The way his cool breath blew across my skin when he treated it. The feel of his thigh pressed against mine while he fumbled with the *blind date with a book* bows and the way it triggered the memory of us sitting on my bed last year right before I kissed him.

And then, when he found the vintage watch? It's as if the universe didn't think I'd been humiliated enough when it comes to Liam Hargrove.

Not only was he up and gone before I woke up, but there was another unsolicited token in my advent calendar this morning. A small, cheesecloth pouch filled with spices. The second I smelled it, I was reminded of Liam and our conversation last year about mulled wine.

The bell above the door rings, and my heart does a traitorous little skip.

Another person that is not Liam enters, so I help them find the monster romance series they're looking for, then return my focus to reshelving the historical romance section.

I'm wearing the blush hairbow again. Not because Liam liked it, but because I think it's cute.

I spend the afternoon organizing the back room to make the restock later this week easier for me and Charlotte. During my break, I check my email and notice a new message from *PourChoices*.

*PourChoices: How's it going with the interloper?*

*JuniReads: Funny you should ask. He's nowhere to be found.*

*PourChoices: So, you're having a good day without him?*

I want to say everything is great without Liam lurking around the stacks of my bookstore, but it would be a lie.

*JuniReads: I keep expecting him to pop up behind a shelf with a smug comment and a pastry. It's unsettling not being unsettled.*

*PourChoices: Sounds like you miss him.*

*JuniReads: I do not miss him...I might miss the pastries.*

*PourChoices: Pastries and smug comments. That's a very specific craving.*

I snap my laptop shut before I can type something I'll regret. I've already pushed the boundary of the business forum relationship with *PourChoices*, so I should probably stop sharing silly personal grievances I have with him.

Besides, I need to forget about Liam and focus on what is important. My store. The holidays. Celebrating with my family.

He can do whatever he wants.

I don't care.

Not at all.

Outside of putting up the tree, decorating gingerbread houses is my favorite holiday tradition.

And in true Jensen family fashion, we make it a big deal.

A loud, over-the-top decorating party that culminates in a vote for the best of the best. With categories including "Most Likely to be Condemned by the HOA," "Best Use of Candy in a Non-Candy Way," "Architectural Ambition Award," and "Best in Snow" which usually goes to the child that drowns their house in five pounds of frosting.

After a hectic day at the store and spending an unacceptable amount of time thinking about Liam even though I absolutely shouldn't be, I'm desperate for this. Family chaos. Sugar. A chance to reset my scrambled brain.

But as luck would have it, I get caught at the store after hours working on the agenda for the Books & Bubbly event, and by the time I'm juggling the crockpot of mulled wine I made this afternoon, I don't even have time to change out of my coffee-stained sweater.

Who cares? It's just my family. No one there to impress.

I force myself to ignore the mental image of Liam in a towel.

*He probably won't even be there.*

But if he isn't, where is he?

When I walk into my parents' house, I'm hit with that instant holiday rush. The scent of pine and gingerbread. My mom's multiple Christmas trees. A million twinkle lights. And Nat King Cole crooning from the stereo.

I inhale the magic and start to relax.

Then I see *him*.

Standing by the fireplace in a dark green sweater that fits him way too well, laughing with my dad and Jasper. A plate of gingerbread cookies in hand like he belongs here.

I wobble, nearly dropping the crockpot of mulled wine, but manage to make it into the kitchen.

There, Cassie greets me then lifts the lid and sniffs, her nose scrunching. "Who actually drinks this stuff? It's basically hot potpourri."

"It's festive," I argue.

Clearly, Cassie did not put the mulled spice bag in my advent calendar. And if she did, she's regretting it.

Mom appears with a tray of appetizers and sweeps me into a hug. She pulls back, frowning at my hand. "Is that a burn?"

"Hot cocoa spill. I'm fine," I mumble, but she's still frowning.

Her eyes flick to the bow in my hair instead. "I love this one. Where'd you find it?"

I open my mouth, then shut it again. Because no one is fessing up to my advent calendar surprises and it's making me crazy.

"Um—" I start, but before I can make something up, my cousin's kids barrel through the kitchen, grab fistfuls of gumdrops off the decorating table, and vanish in a trail of squeals and sugar dust.

Mom gestures toward the lone gingerbread kit at the end of the table. "We saved you the last one."

I glance at Cassie hopefully. "You want to build with me?"

"Sorry, already teamed up with Wiley," she says. "It was basically *Mr. & Mrs. Smith* but with royal icing and passive-aggressive gumdrops."

Mom pats my arm like she's about to drop a bomb. "So, you'll be with Liam."

"Liam?" I choke.

And right on cue, as if he was summoned, he appears at my shoulder.

"Hey, Firefly." His voice is low against my ear. Warm. Infuriating. Intimate.

"Firefly?" my mom echoes, perking up.

Liam smiles, all bright-eyed and obnoxiously charming. "Juniper's new nickname. For her bright smile and radiant presence."

"Oh, that's adorable."

My mom and Cassie blink up at Liam like he's the most thoughtful man.

"Is that mulled wine?" Liam asks, grabbing a cup. "I love this stuff." He winks at me, and I nearly combust.

Cassie presses her lips together. "So does Juni."

My mom leaves to refresh her drink, and Cassie decides to join Wiley and a few others in a game of holiday charades.

"I didn't know you'd be here," I mutter.

"Jasper invited me."

Of course he did.

I jab a carrot in the spinach dip.

"How was your day?" I ask, trying for casual.

His eyes flick to my bandaged hand before he answers. "Good. Made some calls, sat in on a meeting with Jasper. Nothing too wild."

"Hmm." I bite the carrot in half; aware I'm basically vibrating with irritation.

His lips twitch. "Did you miss me?"

"Absolutely not."

"Not even my expert bagging skills?"

"Charlotte's back," I sniff. "I survived."

He dips his head, lowering his voice so only I can hear. "You sure about that?"

My mom's voice cuts in before I can fire back. "Liam, you don't mind helping Juniper with the house, do you? With her burn, she'll need an extra pair of hands."

Liam beams at me like this is the greatest Christmas gift he could get. "I'm all hers."

And before I can argue, he slides an arm around my back, steering me toward gumdrops, frosting bags, and utter ruin.

# TWELVE
## LIAM

THE JENSENS' festively decorated living room feels like a portal back to last Christmas Eve when the realization that I had feelings for my best friend's sister hit me like a lightning strike. The memory of Juniper's lips soft and sweet against mine, and how I was too much of a coward to claim what I wanted.

She shifts beside me now, our elbows brushing as she steadies the chimney I'm propping up with a candy cane. She's pretending to be annoyed about building this thing with me, but her focus is all in and I can't help but be charmed by how serious she takes a frosting battle.

"You're weirdly good at this," she says, brow furrowed as she presses a gumdrop into place.

"At one point, I wanted to be an architect."

She pauses, surprise flickering across her face. "Really?"

I nod, adding another swirl of icing along the roofline. "My parents are both architects. It was the plan. Until it wasn't."

"I didn't know that."

"There's a lot you don't know about me, Firefly."

She breaks eye contact to reach for the tray of candy, her sleeve brushing my arm, the faint scent of sweet plums and something warm drifting my way.

When I finish the roof seam, she gently presses the two pieces together. She does it delicately, mindful of the bandage on her hand. I want to tell her to stop, to let me do the tricky parts, but I know better than to tell Juniper Jensen she needs help she doesn't want.

"We have to beat Stella and Jasper." Her voice drops conspiratorially. "They can't have everything. They're disgustingly in love, they're engaged, they're probably going to win the 'Architectural Ambition' award just for existing."

I grin at her little rant. "So, sabotage?"

"Not sabotage. Just ruthless, festive competition." She points her piping bag at me like a wand. "Don't mess this up, Hargrove."

"Noted." I lean closer, careful not to bump her burnt hand. "Whimsical theme, right? Lots of pink?"

She gives me a suspicious look, glancing down at her blush turtleneck and the matching bow in her hair. "You notice way too much."

"I'm observant. It's a gift."

She rolls her eyes but her mouth twitches, betraying the smile she's fighting.

I cut tiny windows into the gingerbread walls, then shape miniature book spines out of modeling chocolate. When I press them into the "windowsill," she laughs. It's a soft, bright sound that punches straight through my ribs.

"Of course you made it a bookstore." She shakes her head. "You're insufferably charming when you want to be."

I lean in to murmur, "You like it, though."

She glares but doesn't deny it.

Her mom pops by to check our progress. "How's it coming, you two?"

"Masterpiece in progress," I say, earning a conspiratorial nod from Juniper's mom.

"It's going to be the best one yet," Juniper adds. Her smile for her mom is warm, but I see the truth in the tight line of her shoulders. She's fighting not to melt around me.

When her mom drifts away, I glance at the candy tray. There, one lone cherry swirl candy sits in the corner. I know exactly why she's eyeing it.

"Don't even think about it," she warns.

"It's the perfect wreath for the front door."

"It's my favorite." She reaches for it at the same time I do.

Our hands collide. Her bandaged one ends up resting lightly on top of mine and I catch the quick hiss she tries to hide.

"Easy." I brush my thumb gently along the uninjured edge of her knuckles. "You should rest that hand, Firefly."

She huffs. "You're impossible."

"I think you like it."

Before either of us can claim the candy, one of her cousin's kids zooms by and snatches it, giggling with triumph as they run off.

Juniper's jaw drops. "Did you see that?!"

I deadpan, "They clearly hate you."

"You did this. You jinxed my candy."

"Guess we'll have to make do with the peppermint."

"I wasn't going to decorate with it. I was going to eat it."

When her mom calls for the final judging, Juniper looks at our crooked, candy-raided gingerbread bookstore, then back at me. And for just a second, under the twinkle lights and layers of frosting, it feels like she's not mad at all.

❄

"This year's winner of the *Sweetest Love Shack* goes to..." Julie holds the slip of paper aloft like she's about to announce an Oscar. "Juniper and Liam!"

Juniper lets out a little squeal that makes my chest tighten. She jumps, literally jumps, then throws her arms around my neck. For a heartbeat, she's pressed up against me, all warm sweetness and soft hair and bright, victorious laughter.

Then she realizes what she's doing. Her big, startled eyes meet mine and she quickly drops her arms, giving my chest an awkward pat like she's congratulating a coworker, not a man she once asked to take her virginity.

"Good job," she says stiffly, avoiding my grin as she slips away into the kitchen.

I'm still standing there when Jasper and Stella find me.

"Nice work, man," Jasper says, clapping me on the shoulder.

"Thanks, but that was all Juniper." I watch her weaving through her family, hugging her mom, laughing with her cousin's kids like I'm not standing here wanting more.

Stella gives me a knowing look. "So...how's our girl handling your extended stay?"

Jasper eyes my sweater which is mostly icing-free except for a smear near my wrist.

"You're not covered in frosting, so I assume you're not dead yet."

I huff a dry laugh. "I'm surviving. But I'm starting to understand why you looked so damn miserable all those years."

Jasper lifts a brow. "Miserable?"

"You know what I mean. You were in love with Stella

while pretending you weren't." I rake a hand through my hair, eyes tracking Juniper as she tries to duck behind the snack table. "I feel like that guy in that movie Stella made us watch."

Stella smirks. "You're going to have to be more specific. I've made you guys watch a lot of movies."

"The one where the guy can't just be friends with the girl. Where he realizes he wants her and wants the rest of his life with her to start now."

Stella's smile softens. "*When Harry Met Sally*."

"Yeah. That one. I'm Harry." I drag a palm over my jaw. "Except instead of a New Year's Eve confession, I've got gingerbread houses and forced proximity to work with."

Jasper chuckles. "You're going to need to do better than icing and mulled wine, man."

"I know." I glance toward Juniper one more time—pink bow slightly askew, cheeks flushed from laughing—and my gut twists with the need to close the space she keeps wedging between us.

"I need something," I murmur, more to myself than to them. "Something to tip the scales."

Stella squeezes my arm. "You'll figure it out, Liam. She's stubborn, but you're impossible."

"Good thing that's always worked for me."

# THIRTEEN
## JUNIPER

THE KITCHEN'S mostly dark now, lit only by the soft glow of the under-cabinet lights. Everyone else has moved downstairs to the oversized sectional to watch a holiday movie.

Noting the mulled wine I brought is gone, I unplug the crockpot and run the ceramic insert under the faucet to soak it. I'm tidying up the gingerbread house displays when I catch the shimmer of a cellophane wrapper. I'd been certain, from the way they'd been bouncing off the walls, that the kids had eaten every last piece of candy, but the universe must know I'm in need of a sweet treat and left me one cherry swirl hard candy to enjoy.

Pinching the ends of the cellophane wrapper between my fingers, I pull them apart to release the candy.

"What do you have there?"

The voice startles me, and the spiral burgundy and white candy skitters across the countertop. My eyes dart toward the doorway where Liam has appeared. He's leaning there, arms crossed, grin lazy. The kind of grin that makes me want to throw something at his perfect face.

Or kiss it.

*Oh, hell no.*

He's trying to distract me, but I'm not playing to lose. Not like last year.

I smack my hand down on the candy piece to claim it.

Liam pushes off the doorframe. "Is that a cherry swirl candy?" he asks, eyes flashing with curiosity as he approaches.

"Yeah. And it's mine." I teasingly hold it in his direction before dramatically popping it into my mouth.

Cherry creamy goodness. It's so delightful, I nearly moan. Maybe this day is getting better after all.

He takes a step toward me. "You sure about that?"

"Uh, yeah." I suck hard on the candy, then let it slide across my tongue so the flavor bursts, causing my mouth to water. "It's in my mouth."

He raises a brow. "Is that supposed to stop me?"

I narrow my eyes, my cheeks hollowing around the candy. "You wouldn't dare."

"Oh, Firefly," he murmurs, "you must not know how seriously I take a dare."

He's right in front of me now, too close. The kitchen suddenly feels much smaller, the countertops too narrow to hide behind.

I straighten my spine, refusing to retreat. "What exactly are you planning to do? Wrestle it out of my mouth?" I laugh because the thought is outrageous, and I can't even comprehend Liam doing it.

He leans in, his eyes locked on mine, the corner of his mouth twitching with amusement. "Maybe."

I take a step back, only for my hip to bump the counter. No more escape routes.

"You can't be serious."

His gaze drops to my lips. "That's the thing, Firefly. When it comes to you, that's exactly what I am."

My brain is reeling from his words, trying to find an explanation because he can't mean that.

Before I can stop him, he swoops in, one hand bracing beside me on the counter, the other catching my waist just enough to pull me forward. His mouth hovers over mine—not quite kissing, but close enough that I feel the warmth of his breath.

I tighten my jaw around the candy, determined.

"Oh my god, are you seriously going to tongue-wrestle me for a piece of candy?" I squeak, my voice high and breathless.

"I take my desserts very seriously," he murmurs against my lips.

His lips brush mine once. Just a graze. A tease. My breath stutters.

I'm dying for more, but I don't want him to know it. He's teasing me, and while it's thrilling, it's dangerous, too. The line between flirting and falling hard. Besides, I can't let it be easy for him.

But then he's looking at me like I'm the only thing in the room that matters, and it makes it hard to remember all the reasons I built the wall in the first place.

I tilt my chin, trying to look unaffected, even as my heart launches into a sprint.

"This how you win candy fights?" I ask, my voice low and breathy. "By stealing kisses that aren't yours?"

He smirks, but there's heat in his eyes now. A flicker of something more serious beneath the grin. "Only when I want the prize this badly."

My heart squeezes. *Are we still talking about the candy?*

Then he tilts his head and captures my mouth.

Suddenly it's a tug-of-war with our mouths, the candy sliding between us, rolling between our tongues.

My pulse spikes.

It's ridiculous and heated and funny. And holy hell, electric.

We're grappling now.

I twist in his arms, trying to keep the candy from him. Laughing through my protests, but he's quicker, his arm gripping tighter around my waist as he tilts my chin up and presses deeper into my mouth.

I gasp, stunned. But it only aids him in taking what he wants.

The cherry swirl candy and another lick of my mouth. He easily steals the candy with a cocky swipe of his tongue.

He pulls back slowly, grinning, lips stained the faintest pink. His tongue darts out, and when it does, I see it.

The candy sitting right there on his tongue.

That smug, infuriating ass.

My eyes narrow.

"Oh, you think you've won?" I scoff.

He raises a brow, daring me. "Pretty sure the scoreboard says—"

I don't let him finish. I surge forward, fisting the front of his sweater, and kiss him like I mean it. Like I'm the one calling the shots now. And I would be if I didn't suddenly get wrapped up in the feel of him against me. The feel of his hot mouth on mine. The way his fingertips dip beneath my sweater, teasing the sensitive skin above my waistband.

*Wait. What was this all for?*

*Oh, yeah, the candy.*

I press in farther, then drag my teeth against Liam's bottom lip.

A sound resonates from low in his throat, surprised and undone.

My tongue sweeps into his mouth, claiming the candy, and maybe a little piece of him, too.

I lean back slowly, smug as hell, and pop the candy between my teeth. "Thanks for holding that for me."

Liam just stares at me, completely wrecked, lips kiss-swollen and chest rising fast.

And if I weren't feeling the exact same way, I'd probably enjoy it even more.

"There you two are." My mom's voice cuts through the moment like a snowplow down Founders Street.

I jolt back a step, nearly choking on the candy. Liam straightens too fast and knocks his hip into the counter, swearing under his breath.

With a clipboard in hand, my mom, in her red cardigan and jingle bell earrings, looks like she's about to direct a Christmas play.

"Yup. It's us. Two holiday roomies. Just hanging out in the kitchen."

Her eyes narrow for a moment, like she's onto us, but then she waves a hand.

"I'm planning a surprise engagement dinner for Jasper and Stella, and I need you two to help me pull it off."

I glance at Liam. He's already watching me.

As if the atmosphere wasn't already warmer than chestnuts roasting, my mom just tossed us straight into the fire.

"What did you have in mind?" I ask.

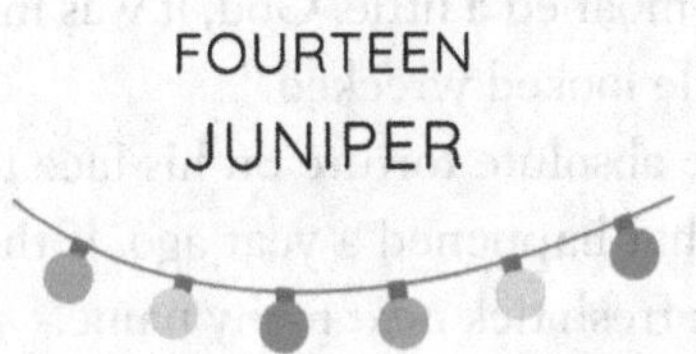

# FOURTEEN
## JUNIPER

CASSIE YANKS a sequined tree skirt off the rack and holds it up like a prize. "Yay or nay?"

I blink at it, then at her. "What?"

Cassie narrows her eyes. "That's what I thought. You're barely here right now. Earth to Juniper. What happened? You look like you got hit by a Hallmark truck full of unresolved tension."

I open my mouth, then close it. My lips tingle. I can still feel it. *Feel him.*

"Okay, don't freak out," I say—which is exactly the kind of sentence that makes Cassie drop everything she's holding.

"Oh my god. You kissed Liam."

"No! I mean...technically, he kissed me. But only to steal candy from my mouth. So, it doesn't count. Except...it kind of does." I groan. "It was—"

"Hot." Cassie finishes for me, a wicked grin pulling at the corners of her mouth.

"Yes," I whisper, glancing around like the Christmas tree décor aisle might be bugged. "Ridiculously hot. Like, I forgot what year it was. My knees went soft. And then I kissed him back. To steal it back."

"You kissed him back?" she practically shrieks.

"No, I kissed him. Like, leaned in, full mouth, took the candy, maybe moaned a little. God, it was insanely hot." My lips twitch. "He looked wrecked."

Seeing the absolute torture on his face took some of the sting out of what happened a year ago. If there was a score-card, I've got a fresh tick next to my name.

I fan my face. My skin still burns.

Cassie drops the tree skirt in the cart. "Juni. You minx."

"Don't give me that look. It wasn't supposed to happen. I was just being flirty. I mean it was petty revenge-flirty. And then he kissed me like I was something he'd been dying to taste again."

Cassie's eyes go wide. "Did you kiss for *real*-real?"

I exhale. "It felt real. Which is the problem."

Because now every cell in my body hums when he's near. I woke up this morning with my lips still swollen, my heart thudding too hard every time I thought about how his fingers slid along my jaw. How close he'd gotten. How I almost forgot everything I'm supposed to protect when it comes to Liam. Like my barely mended heart.

And then, the kicker.

"This morning," I say, voice dropping. "There were cherry swirl candies in my advent calendar."

Cassie blinks. "Like the candy he stole from your mouth?"

I nod. "Exact same kind. And I didn't put them there. You didn't either, right?"

"Unless I blacked out during our Christmas movie marathon last week." She arches a brow. "You think it was him? Like, he's been sneak-gifting you?"

"I don't know. But it feels like too much of a coincidence."

What I don't say: If Liam is behind the advent calendar, then maybe he didn't just walk away last year. Maybe he's been here the whole time. Wanting. Regretting. Taking action now.

But if I let myself believe that, and I'm wrong? It'll wreck me.

"I just—" I stop. "If it's him, what does it mean? Is it a game? Does he regret rejecting me? Or is it just fun?"

Cassie wraps her arm around my shoulders. "Do you want it to mean something?"

That's the thing. I'm not sure. But my stupid heart already does.

"I—"

"A little advice from someone who's weathered the Liam Hargrove crush and all its aftermath with you?" Cassie says, voice soft but fierce. "Don't overthink it."

I blink. "That's your advice?"

Cassie nods solemnly. "Yes. Because I've seen you spiral. And that's not what we're doing this year.

"Juni." She squeezes my shoulder. "You don't have to solve him. Or label this. Or build a ten-year plan. Maybe it's not about figuring out if he's your forever."

I hesitate. "Then what is it about?"

"It's about you wanting him. Remember? A year ago, you were okay with just sex. And clearly, he wants you now. So maybe, just let it be fun. No expectations."

"No expectations." I repeat it, tasting the words. They feel foreign, dangerous, and kind of delicious. I let out a slow breath. "You think I can do that?"

"Get what you want, Juni. And if he leaves again, make

sure he doesn't take anything with him you weren't willing to give."

I nod, more to convince myself than anything.

No strings. No plans. Just stolen kisses and bad decisions wrapped in tinsel. I can survive that...right?

After I finish shopping with Cassie, I drop her off at her parents', then drive over to my family's house.

This year is different in many ways. The fact I'm not living at home anymore, but also with Jasper and Stella together now, it will forever change the landscape of our family holidays. Luckily, Stella's family lives across the street so there's no need for them to commit to one family vs. the other when it comes to spending time for holidays and special occasions.

And, I love seeing Jasper happy, but I miss our time together. Just two siblings teasing each other.

I swing open the back door of my parents' house with a box of decorations balanced on my hip, only to find Jasper at the kitchen table, intently looking at his laptop like a man possessed.

"Please tell me you're not working," I say, nudging the door closed with my foot.

"I'm not," he says without looking up. "Well, not technically."

I round the kitchen island to squint at his screen. "Are you seriously looking at wedding venues?"

He finally glances up, pushing his glasses up his nose. "Don't judge me."

I set the box down with a thud. "I'm not judging. I'm

just deeply impressed by the speed at which you've become that guy."

"What guy?"

"The guy who makes a wedding Pinterest board before the proposal glitter has even settled."

Jasper scoffs. "This is practical. If we don't start looking now, we'll end up getting married next to a gas station in off-season Wyoming."

I lean on the counter, grinning. "I mean, Stella would make a stunning bride in front of a convenience store slushie machine."

"She said I could browse," he mutters. "As long as I don't do anything until after Christmas. She doesn't want to steal focus from the holiday stuff."

"Wow. Who knew you'd be the eager one in this relationship?"

"I contain multitudes," he says dryly.

For a second, it's easy. Just me and Jasper doing our usual sibling banter. But then I glance at his face—the one that's known me through every awkward phase, every heartbreak.

Which makes me wonder what he would think about me and Liam. Casually, of course. Like Cassie and I decided. Maybe casual means I don't even need to bring it up with Jasper. I've never said a word about my crush on Liam to him. And if Liam and I started hooking up, it's not like I'm going to steal my brother's best friend away from him.

He leans back, stretching his arms overhead. "What brings you by?"

"Mom wanted the vintage Santa mugs. I had them at the store." I pause, then add casually, "Thought I'd say hi."

"Hi," he says, brow lifting. "And?"

"And what?"

"You've got your Juniper face on."

I cross my arms. "What face is that?"

"The one that says 'I have a secret, and I'm trying really hard not to let you pry it out of me.'"

I roll my eyes. "You're imagining things."

He tilts his head. "Does this have anything to do with a certain Liam Hargrove?"

"What? No." My stomach flips. "Why would it?"

"Well, for starters, you've mentioned him approximately zero times despite the fact that he's literally staying in your apartment."

"Not by choice."

He grins. "I know. But I know you, Juni. And I know you don't let just anyone share your space, especially after what happened last year."

"What happened last year?" I feign innocence.

"You and Liam kissed."

"He told you that?"

"Yeah. Then I promptly told him to never mention touching my sister ever again."

I snort. "Good talk."

"It was Hargrove-style emotional cowardice," he says, then softens. "But I also know he regrets it."

I blink. "How do you know that?"

"Because we talk. And because I wouldn't have let him stay with you if I didn't think he deserved a shot to make it right."

My breath catches. "You—what?"

"I gave him the green light," he says simply. "But I told him he'd have to earn it. Earn you."

I glance down at the countertop, suddenly fascinated by a chip in the ceramic tile.

"He messed up," Jasper continues. "You put yourself out there, and he got scared. But I also know he's been carrying that regret around for a year. I've never seen him like this, Juni."

I look up. "Like what?"

Jasper smirks. "Like a man who knows what he wants and is scared to death of not getting a second chance."

I swallow hard, the ache in my chest doing battle with the warmth blooming in my stomach.

"You could've told me," I say, quieter now. "That he talked to you."

He shrugs. "Would it have changed anything?"

Maybe. Maybe not.

But now I know Liam didn't just show up on a whim. He planned this. Thought it through. Talked to my brother.

And Jasper let him in.

Which means now...I have to decide if I will, too.

The room quiets for a beat.

"I don't know if I'm—" I start.

"You don't have to be anything," he interrupts. "Just don't write him off before he's had a chance to show you he's not the same guy who left last year."

I nod slowly, heart thudding in my chest.

He points a finger at me. "And if he screws it up again—"

"I'll kill him," I finish.

Jasper laughs. "Not if I get to him first."

I smile, but there's a tremor in my chest I can't quite hide.

# FIFTEEN
# LIAM

SNOW FLURRIES DRIFT DOWN in that postcard-perfect way, except I'm standing in a drift up to my ankles trying to untangle fifty feet of rogue Christmas lights with fingers that no longer feel attached to my body.

Juniper emerges from the barn wearing a Santa hat she did not have on five minutes ago. It's fuzzy and ridiculous, and when she pushes a strand of hair behind her ear, the pompom bounces like it has its own agenda.

"Don't say it," she warns, bending to grab a strand of lights.

I wasn't going to say anything about the hat. I was too busy trying not to stare at the flush on her cheeks and the way her red coat cinches tight at her waist.

"You look festive," I say innocently.

"You sound smug."

"I'm not." I hand her the end of the string I've been detangling for twenty minutes. "I'm just thrilled to be in the freezing cold doing electrical work with zero credentials."

We've been assigned by Julie Jensen to decorate the

barn at The Frosty Fir tree farm where Jasper and Stella's surprise engagement dinner is to be held tomorrow evening. According to everyone who knows her, Stella loves a good light display. So here we are. Battling the snow and frost and dim lighting to bring a romantic holiday vision to life.

Juniper snorts, then promptly slips on a patch of ice and face-plants into my chest. I wrap an arm around her on instinct.

She freezes, her palms flat against me. Slowly, she leans back just far enough to glare.

"Don't say anything," she mutters again.

"Still wasn't going to," I murmur. "But for the record, I'd catch you every time."

Her eyes flick to mine, and just for a second, the world goes quiet. The wind stills. The lights twinkle. I swear the snow pauses midair.

She clears her throat and shoves the string lights at me like a shield. "Let's go. You better not mess this up. This is for Jasper and Stella."

"I know." I grin. "Very hush-hush surprise dinner. I'm an excellent secret keeper."

She lifts an eyebrow at me. "Speaking of secrets...I talked to Jasper."

My heart thumps. "Yeah?" I try to sound casual but fail miserably.

She fiddles with a bulb that's gone dark. "He said you told him. About last year. About me."

"Did he?" I ask, but she ignores my lame deflection.

"I didn't realize you'd actually *talked* about it," she says, a note of wonder—or maybe confusion—threading her voice.

I shift closer, tucking a loose strand of hair under her hat. "I told him I messed up. That I wanted to fix it."

She looks at me, cheeks pink from more than just the cold. "He said you had to earn it."

"I plan on it," I say quietly.

Her mouth curves, like she's fighting a smile she doesn't want me to see. She rolls her eyes instead, turning away too fast. "Good luck, Hargrove."

Ten minutes later, she's on the ladder, arm outstretched toward a nail while I anchor the base.

"I swear if this ladder tips—"

"I've got you," I say. And I do. In every way.

She stretches higher, the hem of her coat rising just enough to reveal the backs of her thighs in thick tights. I try not to look. I fail miserably.

"I need another clip," she calls down.

I fish one out of my pocket. "Catch."

It smacks her in the chest and disappears into the snow.

She glares down at me. "You're useless."

"You're welcome."

"You're ridiculous."

"You're beautiful."

She goes still. For one beat. Two.

Then she shakes her head like she's shaking the thought of me loose. "Focus, Liam."

Oh, I'm focused. On the way her breath fogs when she laughs. The way she keeps choosing to be near me even when she doesn't want to. The way I'm pretty sure I've never wanted someone more in my life.

She clips the last strand in place, then starts down the ladder.

"Careful," I say, holding out my hands.

"Relax, I'm—"

Her boot slips, but I catch her.

Again.

Now she's pressed to me. Her hands gripping my coat. My arms locked around her waist, her breath hitching just slightly.

"This is getting to be a habit," she whispers.

"You falling for me?" I ask, stupidly hopeful.

Her eyes narrow, but she doesn't move. "I meant the slipping."

"Same thing."

A beat passes. Then she laughs—soft and unexpected—and I swear I feel it in my ribs.

"What?" she says, still in my arms.

I don't say the truth. I can't yet.

Instead, I say, "You're lucky I'm tall."

"You're lucky I haven't shoved you into a snowbank yet."

"I'd take it," I grin. "If it means you'd climb on top of me."

Her mouth falls open in mock scandal.

"You're insufferable."

"You're irresistible."

She doesn't kiss me. But she looks at my mouth like she's thinking about it.

"You're soaked," she says breathlessly, noting my damp coat.

"So are you," I murmur against her ear.

Her breath hitches just as the door to the barn slams shut.

Martin, the Frosty Fir Tree Farm owner, breaks the spell. "You know we have people to do that."

Juniper pulls away, clearing her throat. "My mom insisted. Wanted it to be personal."

"Very personal," Martin deadpans. He raises a brow at

Juniper's hat, then at me, then at the half-done entryway. "Looks good. Stella will love it." He heads back inside without another word, leaving us in the swirl of fresh snow and too much unspoken tension.

I fight a grin while Juniper yanks the Santa hat off and smacks my arm with it.

A moment later her phone buzzes in her pocket. On a sigh, she pulls it out. I watch her expression drop the second she sees the screen.

"Everything okay?" I ask, already knowing the answer is probably no.

"It's Charlotte," she mutters, reading a new text with her teeth worrying her bottom lip. "Now she's sick. Probably caught it from her son. She can't help me tonight."

"Help you with what?" I ask, stepping closer, drawn in despite how hard she keeps trying to shove me out.

"Restock. I have a huge shipment to unpack and shelve before the Books & Bubbly event this weekend. It'll take all night on my own." She tucks her phone away with an exhale that fogs in the cold air. "It's fine. I'll handle it."

I reach for the end of the tangled lights in her gloved hand, coaxing her to look at me. "Not on your own you won't. I'll help."

She arches a brow. "Don't you have plans? Meetings? Something better to do?"

I grin. "Not tonight. Let's finish this, then I'm helping you with the store. Non-negotiable."

Her eyes narrow like she wants to argue, but her shoulders drop a fraction, that unguarded softness slipping through before she hides it again.

"Fine," she mutters. "But if you mess up my display tables, you're dead to me."

I smile at her, ignoring the snow melting into my hair, ignoring the cold numbing my fingers, because the warmth I feel right now has nothing to do with the lights or the barn or the Santa hat bouncing over her forehead.

It's her. It's always been her.

LOGIC WON out and I agreed to let Liam help me restock the store. That traitorous voice in my head didn't realize I'd have to watch his sleeves rolled to the elbows, showing off those ridiculously strong forearms, and the veins that pop every time his big-ass hands grip a book spine before gently coaxing it onto the shelf. It's downright obscene, and I can't stop staring.

Add in the dreamy backdrop of my bookstore's twinkle lights, the smell of pine garland, and the way he keeps smiling at me like I'm the only thing worth noticing. I'm doomed.

I fan myself with a floppy paperback, trying to swallow past the desert in my throat. It feels like I'm standing behind a dam that's about to split wide open. Probably good timing. I need the water.

We both reach for the next stack at the same time. Our hands brush. His touch is warm and sends that buzzy, electric tingle racing up my arm.

Nope. I need a distraction, and fast.

"So," I say, grabbing the nearest book like I'm studying the synopsis. "Do you miss the city?"

He pauses, looking down at me with a lazy grin. "New York?"

I nod, trying for casual. "Yeah. All that noise. Skyscrapers. Coffee on every corner."

He shrugs, sliding another book onto the shelf like he's not aware I'm studying his veins like they're plot twists. "I love it. It's home. But..." He glances around my little store. "This doesn't suck, either."

Something in my chest tugs. Dangerous. I look away quickly, pretending to straighten a stack of bookmarks.

I tell myself this is exactly why I can't let him get under my skin again. Because Liam lives in glass towers and endless subways and twenty-four-hour noise. And I live here. In a small town with frosted windows and neighbors who know too much.

"This one looks interesting." He flips open a page like he might just stand here and read it cover to cover.

"Speaking of books...I want mine back."

He glances down at me, all innocent trouble. "Oh, the annotated one? That's for research purposes."

My eyes narrow. "What do you mean? It's not like you're writing a romance novel."

"No. But I'm trying to understand what you want." He closes the book gently, like we're not in a standoff with the weight of a year pressing down on us. "Highlighting, under-lining, margin notes...very educational. Especially that scene with the mirror."

Heat blasts my face. "Liam."

"What?" He leans closer, and the scent of cedar and crisp snow from our light hanging at the barn earlier clings to his sweater. "I'm just trying to apply myself."

"You're impossible," I mutter, but it's soft, like a confession.

He smiles, softer still. "I don't want to mess it up this time."

That makes something in my chest squeeze painfully tight.

"Last year, I thought I was doing the right thing. But I've read the book now, Juniper." His voice drops lower, honey and regret. "I know better."

My pulse hammers in my throat. "It's not a manual, Liam."

"No," he murmurs. "But if it were, I think this would be the part where the hero finally shuts up and kisses her."

He doesn't move. He's waiting. He's always waiting for me to be ready.

I swallow hard. My heart wants to leap. My brain wants to bolt.

"I told myself I wouldn't let this happen again," I whisper.

"And I told myself I'd make it up to you."

His knuckles skim my jaw, tilting my face to him. I realize too late that my hand is already fisted in the front of his sweater, anchoring him to me like I've already decided.

"I've thought about kissing you a thousand times since that night," he says. "The candy kiss was fun. But now I want to do it right."

It's all I can do not to tilt up and close the space. But something inside me panics at the sweetness, the promise, the risk of it being more than I can handle.

So I grab for the only shield I have left. I force out a laugh that doesn't sound like me. "It's just Christmas, you know. The lights, the twinkle...it makes people do reckless things."

His thumb stills against my jaw, like he feels the lie trembling in my skin. "Is that what you're telling yourself?"

I shrug, my voice too thin. "It makes it easier. To keep this light. No promises. Just holiday fun."

His forehead drops to mine, his breath warm and steady. "If that's what you need, Firefly...fine. Just don't lie about what you want right now."

His lips hover over mine, so close I can feel the way he's holding back. He's waiting for me to cross that last inch.

I want to keep pretending. Keep it safe. Keep my heart locked tight behind old disappointments and excuses.

But I can't. Not with him right here, looking at me like I'm worth every risk.

I press up on my toes until my lips are barely brushing against his.

"I want..." The word slips out against his mouth, my guard cracking wide open. "I want this." Even if it's just for Christmas. Even if it's just this moment. Even if it wrecks me.

JUNIPER'S back hits the bookshelf with a soft thud, the paperback in her hand dropping to the floor, forgotten.

This kiss is different from our tongues fighting over candy. It's not the teasing kind. This one is all hands and hunger. All frustration and unfinished business. Her fingers fist in my sweater, her legs parting just enough for me to slide one of mine between hers, snug and intentional. She rocks forward without even thinking and her legs clench tighter around my thigh.

She gasps, but it turns into a whimper when my hands grip her ass and pull her harder against me.

"Liam. Oh, god."

I wanted to kiss her, but dragging her sensitive clit roughly across my denim-clad thigh seems like a good idea, too.

"You like that, Firefly?" I nip at the corner of her mouth.

"Yes."

"Well, I like these skirts of yours." I let my hands dive beneath said skirt and grip her through the cashmere leggings beneath. "I like how easy they make it to slip my hand beneath and touch you. Just like this."

We lose ourselves in it. Kissing like we're teenagers who just discovered how good it feels. Open mouths, hot breaths. Her nails scrape through my hair and I grip her waist tighter, rolling my hips into hers without shame.

She's arching against me now, chasing friction like it's air, and it makes something sharp and possessive snap loose in my chest.

"You're mine," I mutter, not even meaning to say it out loud.

She moans, biting my bottom lip, then says, "You wish."

She's all stubborn contradictions, but she's pulling me closer, not pushing me away, so I'll take it.

Her body rolls against mine like she's past the point of caring. When she presses down again, a soft, strangled noise escapes her throat that nearly undoes me.

"Right there?" I whisper against her ear.

She nods, fast and desperate. Her hands are gripping my sweater like she needs something to hang on to.

"Use it then," I rasp, dragging my mouth down her neck, kissing along her jaw. "Ride my thigh, Firefly. I want to feel you come just like this."

"I—I can't—" she chokes out.

"Yes, you can, baby," I encourage against her ear. "Grind that sweet cunt on my thigh until you shatter."

Her breath stutters at the command. "Liam—"

"You're so close already, aren't you?" My hands grip her hips tighter, guiding her movements with just enough pressure to make her whimper. "Don't hold back now."

Her body goes taut, breath catching, and then she falls apart against me with a soft, bitten-off cry, still grinding down against me like she never wants the feeling to end.

I hold her through it, chest heaving, my own body so wired I'm half afraid I'll lose it, too.

But watching her fall apart for me, because of me, is more satisfying than anything else.

When her legs finally stop trembling, I kiss the corner of her mouth and whisper, "You're mine, Juniper. Whether you're ready to admit it or not."

## EIGHTEEN
## JUNIPER

I'M BUZZING THIS MORNING. Horny, restless, agitated energy hums under my skin like I plugged myself into a Christmas bulb socket. I can't even focus on my audiobook while I get ready because every other sentence fades out to make room for him. For last night.

God, last night.

The memory still makes my knees weak. I can't believe I did that. In my bookstore. Liam's ridiculously strong thigh between my legs like I'd been starving for him for a decade. Which, apparently, I have been. But the evidence should not have been left all over his pants. Yet, it was.

And his mouth. Those filthy, perfect words.

*Grind that sweet cunt on my thigh.*

Jesus, I didn't know I'd like it that much. But then again, I do read about dirty-talking heroes for a living, so maybe it shouldn't have shocked me that his filthy mouth made me come so damn fast and hard.

And now? Now I'm left standing here, staring at my coffee pot like it holds answers. What the hell is happening between us?

After the thigh incident, and my meltdown of a climax, we just went back to restocking shelves. Like nothing happened. Like we hadn't just done that. My brain was a blur of *holy shit* and *do not get attached*.

Because there is no us. Not really.

If his rejection last year gutted me, what's it going to feel like when he packs up that perfect accent, that orgasm-inducing thigh, and flies back to his perfect New York City life next week?

I'm reading into it too much. It was just a moment. A wild, hot, filthy moment with a man I've secretly wanted since the day I met him. Nothing more.

My head clears just in time to stop myself from pouring the pot of coffee into my bowl of oatmeal.

*Oh my god, Juniper. Get it together!*

I set everything down and breathe. One step at a time. Coffee in the mug. Oatmeal in the bowl. Sanity somewhere in my body.

When I feel more composed, I drift over to my advent calendar. Now that I'm certain it's Liam who has been sneaking little surprises behind each door, it's become a ritual I both dread and crave.

At least he's not here this morning to watch me open it. The relief I felt when he texted to say he's spending the day snowmobiling with Jasper was almost as satisfying as last night. I need the space. I need a minute to process.

And yet I miss him. His steady presence. His lazy grin. Another reason I can't let myself fall back under his spell.

I crack open today's tiny door and find a small firefly brooch tucked inside. Delicate wings, a swirl of green on its tail.

My heart clenches. It's beautiful. Thoughtful.

Firefly. His nickname for me, whispered like a secret in

the dark. His word for how I glow when I'm happy. How he says he's always seen me—bright and warm and impossible to ignore. And he knows I love to collect little vintage trinkets like this.

It's too much. Too sweet. Too intimate for my desire to keep him at a casual distance.

But I pin it to my sweater right away. Right over my heart. Like I want him there even if I know better.

I spend the morning alphabetizing a stack of holiday romances I've already organized twice. Every time I catch my reflection in the front window, the firefly pin winks back at me, like a dare I'm not ready to take.

The bell jingles above the door and my mom breezes in.

"Brought you sustenance," she announces, like I'm not fully capable of feeding myself.

Though with all the holiday events and the store restock and Liam consuming nearly every waking thought, she might be right.

I accept the egg salad sandwich and bag of chips she pulls from her purse. Unwrapping the sandwich, I see the avocado peeking out and my mouth waters. I love avocado.

Before I can thank her, her phone rings.

It's the default ringtone at an ungodly volume, and it takes her far too long to answer. I'm about to jab the button for her when she bats my hand away and gingerly picks it up.

"Hi, Jasper."

I turn my attention to my sandwich while I wait for her to finish the call, but an audible gasp snaps my head back up.

"Oh, my goodness," she exclaims, clutching her chest. "Liam hit a tree?"

Liam. *Hit a tree.*

A vivid horrifying image flashes through my mind. Liam's body flung from a snowmobile, slamming into a tree trunk like a rag doll. My limbs go numb.

Liam. Hurt.

Injured.

Dead?

Appetite gone, my chest cinches tight, and I think I might throw up.

"What?" I whisper, my voice so thin it barely exists. My gut twists so hard I nearly double over.

"But he's okay?" my mom asks, pressing her lips together when she nods. "Oh, that's good."

He's okay. Not dead. Good.

She keeps nodding, murmuring something I can't hear, but it does nothing to settle the storm inside me.

I stand abruptly, my untouched sandwich forgotten. I grab my purse with shaking hands.

"Juni, where are you—" She starts, but I cut her off.

"Can you watch the store?" I blurt. I don't wait for her to hang up. I'm already grabbing my keys and bolting for the door.

Twenty minutes later, I'm screeching into the parking lot of the Summit County Hospital.

"Take a breath, Juniper," I mutter, trying to calm the thundering in my chest. "Don't kill yourself on the way to check on him."

Liam is okay. He's alive. But that doesn't ease my heart at the thought of what could have happened.

What if he was gone? And I'd been standing there

playing it cool, pretending I didn't care. What's the point of guarding my heart if I could've lost him anyway?

Cranking the steering wheel, I fly into a parking spot. I almost forget to put my car in park and nearly hit another car.

"I'm so sorry!" I call to the startled driver across from me, then slam my door and sprint for the entrance.

I blow through the automatic doors like a woman possessed, the sound of my boots squeaking against the sterile floor echoing through the ER.

"Liam Hargrove?" I pant to the nurse behind the desk.

She looks up from her screen, mildly alarmed. "He was brought in a little while ago. Exam curtain five—right over there."

I barely wait for her to finish pointing before I'm weaving between wheelchairs and IV poles, muttering apologies, while my heart thuds in my ears.

Curtain five. *Please be okay. Please be okay.*

I whip it open and stop cold.

Oh. *Oh no.*

A man, no, a mummy, lies in the hospital bed, fully encased in a head-to-toe body cast. Only his eyes and mouth are visible. His face is battered, and a little puffy. But he's tall, dark-haired, and currently very silent.

"Liam?" I croak, my voice wobbling.

He doesn't answer. Just blinks. Twice.

My eyes fill with tears as I step closer, grabbing the edge of the bedrail. Yes, he's alive, but a full body cast? It's so much worse than I'd imagined.

"Oh my god. I can't believe this happened to you. I—" I let out a shaky laugh. "I'm so mad at you. For scaring me. For being reckless. For kissing me like you did last night and now I can't even touch you."

He still says nothing, just another blink.

That's how we're going to have to communicate now.

Blink once if you need water, twice if you have an itch.

Selfishly, I'm dying for him to touch me. And now he can't. At least not for a while. Ugh. Is the universe punishing me for not leaping into his arms the moment he showed up?

Knowing what I'm about to say will be another hit to the ego, I power through the humiliation anyway.

"Here's the truth, okay?" I say softly, my voice cracking. "You do mean something. You always have. Even when I didn't want you to. Even when I swore I'd let this silly crush go."

From behind me, a throat clears.

If that's the nurse coming to check vitals, it's the worst possible timing.

"Just a minute. I have to get this out," I say, dropping to the chair next to the bed. "That watch you found? It was for you, but it wasn't from Jasper. I picked it out. I saw it at a vintage shop and immediately thought of you." I swipe at a tear sliding down my cheek. "Even after last Christmas, I never stopped thinking about you. I don't know how to stop."

"Firefly."

The deep rumble makes my heart seize. But unless Liam has a talent for ventriloquism, it did not come from the mummy in the hospital bed. It came from behind me.

I turn my head slowly, and there he is—*Liam*. No body cast, no tragedy. He's dressed in snow pants and a sweater, a stitched-up gash on his forehead, and the smuggest fucking grin I've ever seen.

"I meant curtain six," the nurse calls from the hallway. "Sorry! My bad!"

"How long have you been standing there?" I ask.

"Not long." His lips twitch. "But I did hear every word through the curtain."

"Oh my god." I cover my face with both hands.

Swallowing hard, I turn to the man in the hospital bed and whisper, "I'm so sorry." Then, I shoot Liam a hard stare as I move to rush past him.

He reaches for me, pulling me behind the actual curtain six where I see his winter coat is lying across the bed.

I fold my arms. "You look pretty okay for someone who hit a tree."

"My ego took the worst of it."

I practically snort. His ego? Ha! It's got nothing on mine. I'm the idiot who didn't think twice about hauling-ass to the hospital when I thought he was injured. And for what reason? Because I care even if I wish I didn't.

"Five stitches." He points to his brow. "It could scar and the hair might not grow back right."

"Poor thing."

"Mr. Hargrove, your discharge papers." The nurse dips inside the curtained-off room to hand Liam his paperwork. "Check out at the front when you leave."

"Thank you." He smiles at her, but the second she's gone, his eyes come back to me and his grin softens.

He sees it then and his gaze drops to my sweater where the tiny firefly brooch glints under the fluorescent lights. He lifts his hand, brushing a knuckle gently over the pin.

"It looks perfect on you," he murmurs. The teasing edge in his voice is gone. What's left is something warm and sincere that makes my throat tight all over again. "Better than I imagined."

My arms stay stubbornly crossed, but my chest aches. "Don't try to distract me."

His eyes lift to mine, searching, like he wants to say more but can't quite find it yet. Then he shifts closer, his voice soft. "Hey. Come here."

I hesitate, but his hand finds my hip, tugging me the last few inches. I let him, even though my heart is hammering so hard it might break free.

"You came to see me?"

I shrug. "I was in the neighborhood."

He huffs a laugh, but it's soft. Like he doesn't want to break whatever moment this is.

"You said you care about me?"

"I was stressed," I mumble, looking anywhere but at him. "People say odd things under duress."

"Is this the part where you take it all back? Say you were only being nice to a severely wounded man?"

I roll my eyes. "I was trying to give you a reason to live, obviously. Thought it might help. Maybe I'll swing by the other triage stations to see if anyone else needs a little pick-me-up since you obviously don't need it."

Deflecting with humor, I try to step back, but his grip tightens, not letting me go.

His voice drops, low and certain. "Did you forget, Firefly?"

My breath catches.

"Hmm?" I ask, even though I already know what he's going to say.

"You're mine." His voice is fierce and intimate and terrifying in the best way.

He said it last night and now here he's doing it again. Liam trying to claim me when he's done nothing but make me feel uncertain about what he wants.

"You don't get to say that. Not after last year." I swallow. "What happened last night doesn't mean everything is forgotten."

"I know." He brushes his nose against my cheek. "And I hate what I did. Rejecting you like that—I've hated it every day since."

"Then why did you do it?"

His forehead rests against mine, and for a second, he just breathes.

"Because I was scared. Because I didn't want to lose Jasper, and I didn't think I was worth the risk to you. But I was wrong."

I don't answer. I can't.

"It's only five stitches," he says, his lips skimming the corner of my mouth. "But the second I hit the snow, all I could think about was you. Not my head. Not Jasper. You."

His voice turns to a whisper. "Thought about kissing you. Holding you. Thought about pressing inside you for the first time and making you mine for real."

"Liam," I whisper, heart thudding as desire curls tight and hot between my thighs, but with something else tangled in it. More than need and ache, there's hope.

His thumb skims just beneath the hem of my sweater, brushing bare skin as he exhales a shaky breath. "You put yourself out there last year. You told me what you wanted, and I didn't handle it well."

I blink, surprised by the rawness in his voice.

"I was scared," he says, forehead still pressed to mine. "Of screwing everything up. Of not being enough. But I realize now, I did the worst thing anyway. I left you wondering."

I swallow hard, my throat tight.

"This is me putting myself out there," he continues. "This

is my confession. I want you. Not just for now. Not because we're sharing a space or getting tangled up in nostalgia or the ridiculous errands your mom has us doing together."

He pulls back just enough to look at me—really look at me.

"I felt it last year, and I feel it even more now. And I'm done pretending otherwise."

My chest tightens, causing my breath to catch. It's everything I thought I wanted to hear, but it also changes everything.

"Then make me yours, Liam."

He watches me for one breathless beat.

Then two.

Like he's memorizing the moment.

His hand moves from my hip to the small of my back, pulling me flush against him. My lips part on instinct, a soft gasp slipping out as I feel the hard line of him pressed to my stomach.

"We have to be quiet," I whisper, not sure if it's a warning or a challenge.

His lips curl against mine, a slow, dangerous smile. "Then you'll have to be good."

He walks me backward until my ass bumps the one solid wall of this curtained-off space, his mouth capturing mine in a kiss that starts sweet, but quickly deepens. His tongue tangles with mine, coaxing, teasing...claiming.

One of his hands grips my thigh, tugging my leg over his hip so we're completely connected. The other slides up under my sweater, palm warm and steady on my bare skin, before gliding lower, down the front of my leggings.

I gasp softly into his mouth as his fingers slide beneath my underwear, finding me wet.

"Christ, Firefly," he breathes against my jaw. "You're soaked."

A soft moan escapes before I catch it.

His free hand covers my mouth, not to silence me—to *anchor* me. His eyes are locked on mine, pupils wide with lust, reverence, and hunger.

"I've got you, baby," he whispers. "Let me have you."

His fingers stroke through me with expert ease, teasing slow circles against my clit that make my knees tremble. I bury my face in his neck, panting quietly against his warm skin. His toe-curling scent only spurs me on. I bite down gently on the skin at his collarbone to keep from making a sound.

"Last night was perfect, but this?" he murmurs, his finger teasing at my entrance. "I've thought about how much I want this," he fills me with his fingers. "To make you fall apart under my touch."

He's right. Last night was fun, but now, with his fingers thrusting inside me, it's another level of pleasure.

His fingers move with infuriating precision. Like somehow he's studied me. Like he knows exactly what I need and how I need it.

My head tips back against the wall, eyes squeezed shut as I bite down on the sleeve of his sweater to keep quiet. The sounds I want to make would definitely get us kicked out.

"God, Juni," he murmurs, low and wrecked against my neck. "You're so wet for me. You've been like this all day, haven't you? Just thinking about how you got off on my leg last night."

His fingers curl, slow and deep, and I clench around them.

"You're perfect like this. So fucking tight. So ready."

I whimper, a sound I try to swallow.

Maybe this was a bad idea. I've never been touched by Liam like this before. I'm not sure I can keep quiet.

Every nerve in my body feels lit from within.

It's slow and deliberate. Devastating. Like he's savoring every second.

Meanwhile, I'm trembling. On the verge of falling apart.

"You're doing so good for me," he whispers. "Letting me take care of you like this. Just let go, baby. I've got you."

I want to look at him, but I know if I do, if I meet those heated eyes and see what I already feel—how much he wants me, how much he cares—I'll come undone too fast.

But then he leans in, his lips brushing my ear. "Let go, Firefly. Come for me."

And I do.

Right there. With his fingers coaxing me through it, his hand braced on the wall beside my head, and his lips brushing the shell of my ear. It's too much and not enough. It's everything.

I stifle my moan in his shoulder as my body clenches around his fingers, heat and light rippling through me in waves.

When it's over, I melt against him, breathless and stunned, clinging to the fabric of his sweater.

He doesn't say anything at first. Just holds me. Lets me come back to earth.

And that's almost worse—because when Liam touches me like this, sees me like this, I stop being a woman trying to protect her heart. I become the girl who's always wanted him to keep it.

## NINETEEN
## LIAM

JUNIPER FALLING APART in my arms is becoming a regular occurrence. And I love it.

I want this woman in every way possible, and in this moment, it feels like a reality where she's mine is becoming even more inevitable.

She's trembling, tucked against my chest like she's trying to disappear into me. Her breath catches, and I kiss her temple, hoping she can feel how hard I'm trying not to fall to my knees and beg her to be mine in every damn way.

I keep my hand on her lower back, holding her steady as I slowly ease my fingers out of her and right her clothing. I'd be an idiot not to lick her off my fingers—to taste how sweet she is—so that's exactly what I do.

She pulls back, smoothing her hair, while her eyes are still stormy from what we just did. Finally, she looks up at me with a cautious smile. "Try not to look so smug."

I lean forward, dropping my voice low. "I'm the man who just felt exactly how wet your sweet little cunt gets for me. I'm going to be the smuggest bastard you've ever known."

She huffs, but there's a flicker of heat in her gaze that she doesn't hide fast enough.

And I can't stop watching her. Not as she straightens her shoulders. Not as she wraps herself back up in calm sarcasm, pretending like I don't already know how she tastes, how she sounds when she comes on my hand.

I hold the curtain open for her, and she moves past me into the hallway. Seeing all the doctors and nurses moving around, the patients being admitted, makes it even more real how wrapped up in each other we'd been a moment ago.

At the checkout desk we run into Jasper.

If he's shocked to see Juniper, he doesn't show it. He gives her a hug, then leans in and squeezes me on the shoulder.

"How's the forehead?" He nods toward my bandage.

"All stitched up."

"Good. I squared up with the liability insurance at the snowmobile company."

"Thanks for dealing with that."

"I'm glad Juni was here to hold your hand. I know how much of a big baby you can be with needles."

"Hey. I fainted once during a blood draw and that was because I hadn't eaten anything. Low blood sugar is not a joke."

Beside me Juniper laughs, a real genuine laugh, and I feel the pride in my bones.

"You want a ride?" Jasper asks, motioning toward the direction his car must be parked.

"I'm going to go with Juniper, if that's okay?"

He gives me a knowing glance, huffing out a laugh before nodding. "You bet."

"See you later tonight?" I ask.

"Yeah."

After saying our goodbyes to Jasper, Juniper guides me to where her car is parked askew in the lot.

The observation has me tossing her a curious look.

"Don't even say it."

"What?" I ask innocently, opening the door for her before making my way to the passenger side.

I like the way she looks behind the driver's seat. Hands on the wheel, hair still a little mussed, cheeks pink from the cold.

She fiddles with the heat and mumbles, "Don't bleed on the seat, okay?"

"I didn't realize getting five stitches made me a liability."

A memory sneaks up on me.

Last year, me driving Juniper home from the liquor store. She'd laughed at something I said. Her cheeks were flushed, eyes shining. I remember the grip I had on the wheel, the way my knuckles turned white with the effort of not reaching for her. I'd been so caught off guard by my reaction to her, I'd fought it with everything in my body.

Now she's beside me again.

And this time, I've touched her.

Kissed her.

Wrecked her behind a hospital curtain and I want more.

I open my mouth to tell her something when my phone buzzes in my pocket.

I pull it out, glance at the screen and sigh.

"It's Beck."

"Beck? As in your brother?" she asks, glancing over.

"Yeah." I swipe to answer, bracing myself. "Hey, what's going on?"

Beck's voice crackles through the speaker. "I'm about five minutes from Cedar Hollow and I need a place to stay."

"What? Why? I thought you were skiing with friends."

"Got kicked out of the cabin rental in Park City. Don't ask."

"Of course you did." I close my eyes and pinch the bridge of my nose. That's Beck. Charming enough to talk himself into trouble and just reckless enough to never bother talking himself out of it.

Beside me, Juniper hums along with "Last Christmas" playing softly through the speakers, blissfully unaware of the storm about to roll in...my brother.

"Is that Juniper?" Beck perks up, his grin practically radiating through the line. "Tell her I said hi. And that if you screw this up again, I'm taking my shot."

My grip on the phone tightens until my knuckles crack. Beck's always had a way of pushing my buttons. It's practically a sibling sport for him. But tossing out jokes about Juniper while I'm trying to win her back? Not funny. Not for me.

"Over my dead body."

I catch Juniper glancing at me, brows raised in that soft, curious way she has. She doesn't know how many times Beck has managed to wedge himself between my plans just because he can. And she definitely doesn't know how many times I've had to clean up his messes without letting him see it bothered me.

"Everything okay?" she asks gently.

"Just peachy." I force a smile that doesn't reach my eyes.

Beck chuckles on the other end, clearly delighted by my reaction. "Save me a beer, big brother. And tell Juniper I think she's too good for you."

I hang up on him mid-laugh, my jaw clenching tight. She is too good for me but she's still mine. And Beck's timing could not be worse.

# TWENTY
## JUNIPER

I OPEN the door to find a younger, slightly scruffier version of Liam standing there with a duffel slung over his shoulder and absolutely no shame radiating off him.

"Hi," he says, flashing a grin that could short-circuit small appliances. "You must be Juniper."

"And you must be Beck," I say, stepping aside so he can enter my apartment.

Liam is right behind me, greeting his brother with an embrace that is warm yet giving *I might kill you while you sleep* energy.

Beck drops his bag on the floor like he owns the place, eyes immediately finding the stitches above Liam's eyebrow.

"Well, look at you," Beck says, feigning shock. "Usually I'm the one coming home with stitches, not my brilliant older brother. Snowmobile accident, huh? Was this all part of the plan to impress a certain redhead?" He throws me a wink over Liam's shoulder.

Liam rubs at the area lightly and scowls. "If it was, you showing up just ruined it."

I try not to laugh at the banter between them. "Is

showing up unannounced and expecting a place to stay genetic?" I ask, shooting Liam a look.

Beck grins. "You're fun."

"Don't get your hopes up, Firefly," Liam cuts in before I can respond. "This isn't one of your 'why choose' novels."

I raise a brow and smirk, just to mess with him because I'm starting to realize it's a lot of fun to mess with Liam. "There was this really hot one with two brothers..."

Liam groans. "I'm going to regret letting him sleep here, aren't I?"

Ignoring our back and forth, Beck starts to tour my apartment.

"Ooh," Beck says, glancing around. "So this is where the magic happens."

I arch a brow.

"I meant the advent calendar, obviously," Beck adds, deadpan.

"What do you know about my advent calendar?" I glance between the brothers, catching Liam's hard stare in Beck's direction.

"Just that it's pink and glittery and filled with surprises." Beck gives me a once over. "That really could apply to anything in this flat."

Behind me, Liam lets out a groan and mutters, "Don't encourage him."

I motion toward the living room. "You can take the couch. I'll grab you a blanket and some—"

Liam cuts in. "He can take the guest room."

I blink. "That's *your* room."

Liam shrugs, unbothered. "Not anymore."

My stomach does a somersault. "So where do you plan on sleeping?"

His pointed look is both innocent and full of sin. "With you."

My jaw drops. "Excuse me?"

"I meant—" he holds up both hands, grinning now, "I'll take the floor in your room. Obviously. Unless you've got a curtain we can use to divide the space?"

My eyes narrow at his callback to what just happened between us behind the curtain at the hospital.

Beck drops onto the couch with a wide smile, popping a cherry swirl candy from the bowl on the coffee table into his mouth. "Don't mind me. I'm just a weary traveler in need of shelter and maybe *The Grinch Who Stole Christmas* playing softly in the background. The newer version with Benedict Cumberbatch. Man, I love that one."

"You're a menace," Liam mutters, heading down the hallway.

I watch him go, heart racing as I realize Liam's going to be in my room tonight.

Our forced proximity living situation just leveled up to only one bed.

If I thought having Liam in the room next to mine was overwhelming, the moment he rolls his suitcase into my bedroom, my stomach flutters with nerves.

"Maybe I'll sleep on the couch." I go to leave, but Liam reaches for my hand, pulling me back.

"Hey," he drops his gaze to mine. "I don't expect anything to happen here."

"Good," I say, my voice bright and brittle. "Because I can't say it will."

He nods, but there's that ghost of a smirk at the corner of his mouth, like he knows exactly how full of shit I am. "Of course."

When I walk over to my closet, I check my reflection in

the full-length mirror to make sure my pants aren't on fire. You know, since I'm such a fucking liar.

I do want Liam, and I'm sure he knows it.

But this time? He's going to have to work for it.

I glance back at him standing in my bedroom, looking at home in a way that makes my chest squeeze tight. He's worth wanting. He's worth hoping for.

And maybe, just maybe, he's about to prove he's worth trusting again, too.

Beck is already holding court at the bar five minutes after our arrival at Stella and Jasper's engagement dinner. Giving hugs to people he's never met and complimenting the Christmas tree Liam and I decorated like it's a guest of honor.

He's chaotic and charming, making Liam, who I've always imagined to be the life of the party, look tame.

"Wow," he says to no one in particular. "Smells like cookies, cinnamon, and lifelong emotional commitments. I love this place."

I eye him, trying not to laugh. "You're laying it on thick."

"Can't help it," Beck says, eyes twinkling as he leans toward me. "I'm in a romantic setting with a beautiful woman. I'm just doing my part to raise the stakes."

Liam brushes past us with a narrowed look. "Beck. Try behaving for five minutes."

"I'm charming, not dangerous," Beck replies, winking at me.

I abandon the jousting Hargrove brothers to see if my mom needs any help. She asks me to do a final décor check before Jasper and Stella arrive. It gives me the perfect excuse to focus on the decorations—twinkly lights and garlands wrapped around the wooden barn's posts, but my eyes keep dragging back to Liam. He's helping my aunt and cousin set platters on the buffet. He's wearing that dark green sweater I love. The one that hugs his arms. The one that makes my heart do silly, fluttery things.

And then there's Beck, at my side again, offering me a glass of champagne with a low, "Wouldn't want you to drink alone."

"You're very committed to this bit," I laugh.

"Oh, sweetheart," he says with a grin, "this isn't a bit. But I do like watching Liam's eye twitch when I get too close to you."

From across the room, Liam shoots Beck a sharp look while I take a sip of champagne.

Stella and Jasper arrive and seeing their surprised and grateful expressions makes my chest squeeze. Watching them together reminds me of how far they've come. From childhood rivals at each other's throats to falling in love last Christmas and now engaged.

But Jasper always knew. He wanted Stella and was willing to rearrange his entire life to make sure he didn't lose her again. He moved his whole company to New York before she even knew how he felt. That's the kind of certainty I crave. Someone who picks me, out loud, without hesitation.

Jasper clinks the edge of his glass to get the table's attention.

"First of all, thank you all for being here tonight to celebrate me and Stell. No matter where I've lived or traveled, Cedar Hollow has always been home. Getting to celebrate something this big, at this time of year, with all of you—it means everything."

He looks at Stella, eyes soft.

"Stella has always had my heart. Since that first day in second grade. I just didn't know what it was then. And while it took us twenty years to get here, I wouldn't change a moment of it. She challenges me. She makes me better. And I can't wait for a lifetime of being outwitted, outmatched, and thoroughly humiliated at Skee-Ball."

Laughter erupts around the table.

"But really, a year ago, I moved my whole life across the country because sometimes you don't wait for the right moment, you just pick the person and make every moment count."

He lifts his glass.

"To Stella...Sparky...my North Star. And to all of you, may you find the person who feels like home and never be afraid to build your life around them."

My eyes fall on Liam.

He says I'm not just a for now thing and he means it; I can feel it in the way he looks at me like he'd burn the world down to keep me close. But what does that actually look like? He lives in New York. I'm here. He's Jasper's best friend and business partner. He's always been the guy who keeps things tidy and unmessy. Except, I guess, when it comes to me.

Do we do long distance? Do I uproot my life? Does he uproot his?

Or do we get caught up in this Christmas snow globe and pretend it'll all work itself out when the decorations come down?

I don't know.

But I know I'm not ready to look away.

Beck, seated beside me, clears his throat and leans in. "So, Juniper, if Jasper and Stella are the blueprint, do you think that means we're next?"

I blink. "I think I'd need your middle name first."

He grins. "Trouble. Beck Trouble Hargrove."

Across the table, Liam raises an eyebrow. His wineglass pauses midair. "Pretty sure it's Everett."

Beck shrugs. "Everett is what's on my driver's license. Trouble is more of a lifestyle."

He nudges my shoulder. "Right, Juni?"

I laugh, because it's ridiculous. Because Beck is charming in the way younger siblings of heartbreakers always are: unbothered, bold, and just chaotic enough to make things interesting.

But when I glance across the table again, I nearly choke on my sip of wine.

Liam's jaw is tight. His knuckles are white around his fork. His eyes—those dark, stormy, steady eyes—are locked on me with a look that could melt fresh snow.

Beck leans closer, stage-whispering in my ear. "He's going to throw a dinner roll at me."

I snort.

Liam doesn't throw a dinner roll.

But he does lean forward slightly, resting his elbows on the table, and says in a deceptively casual tone, "You always go for the ones who hide behind jokes?"

Beck grins. "She *used* to."

Liam's eyes never leave mine. "That so?"

My cheeks heat, but I hold his gaze. "Beck's just entertaining me."

Liam lifts his glass. "Well, let me know when you're ready to be done with the warm-up act."

Beck clutches his chest. "Wounded."

I smile into my wineglass. Because I can feel the fire now crackling between us, consuming all the space between right now and the night ahead.

I glance across the table again, and Liam's still watching me.

Not just watching—claiming. Quietly, steadily, like he already knows how this ends and he's just waiting for me to realize it, too.

And something about it—the tension, the hunger, the fact that I'm no longer the only one feeling all of it—sends a pulse of heat through me so sharp I have to shift in my seat.

Last year at this time, I was trying not to cry into my cocoa while Cassie kept the snacks and romcoms flowing.

Liam had crushed me.

Now?

He's watching me like he wants to ruin me—in the best way.

And I'm enjoying it.

The control. The flirtation. The fact that I'm not the only one caught in this web anymore.

This is my revenge arc. My holiday rom-com power play. And the best part?

Liam has no idea I'm just getting started.

I tuck my hair behind my ear and lean toward Beck slightly—just enough to make Liam's eye twitch—and whisper, "So what's your stance on mistletoe?"

Across the table, Liam's fork clinks against his plate like a warning bell.

And for the first time in a year, I feel like I'm the one in control.

I'M BARELY HOLDING it together as I park the car in front of Juniper's flat.

Juniper's laugh is still echoing in my ears. The sight of her pressed shoulder to shoulder with my brother, that flirty little smirk on her lips, the way she leaned in just to watch me twitch. I've been climbing the walls in silence all night.

She's having fun. Which would be fine, great even, if she weren't using my own damn brother to get under my skin. Doesn't she know? She's already there. Been there for a year now and it's time for me to show her exactly what she does to me.

Outside her flat, Beck stretches dramatically. "Okay. What's next? Should we hit the bar? Juni, I bet you're a good pool player. You've got good wrist control."

Juniper bites back a laugh.

I grip the door to her flat building a little harder than necessary. "Actually," I say, calmly, *too* calmly, "I think you're going to crash early, Beck."

He blinks. "What? No way. I've got energy for days. We should go out."

"You should go out," I tell him pointedly, blocking the doorway. "We'll catch up with you tomorrow."

His eyes flick from me to Juniper, who has the audacity to be smirking again, then back to me.

Beck raises his hands. "Right. Copy that. Message received. I'll just..." He gestures vaguely down the street. "Disappear."

"Excellent choice."

I open the door, then after ushering Juniper in, slam it behind us.

Silence.

Juniper stands at the foot of the stairs, that smug little smile pulling at her mouth again.

"Subtle."

I take a slow step toward her. Then another. Her eyes widen, but she doesn't move.

"I've spent all night watching you flirt with my brother," I murmur, voice low. "Letting him whisper in your ear. Letting him make you laugh."

She shrugs innocently. "I didn't let him. He's funny."

"Oh, he's dead."

She tips her head, eyes dancing. "He said you were wound up. Guess he was right."

I'm in front of her now, hands braced on either side of the railing. "I'm wound up because I've spent hours watching the woman I want let someone else pretend to be in my place."

She blinks up at me, her breath catching when I lean in. But I don't kiss her. Not yet. I want her dizzy with it. I want her squirming with the awareness that I'm holding back.

"I've had to sit across from you all night pretending I didn't want to drag you out of that chair and kiss you silly in front of everyone." I press closer, mouth at her ear. "I'm about to make you forget anyone else was ever in the room."

Her smug expression falters. "You're not good at subtle."

"That's right," I say, inching closer. "I'm good at showing up late. At not saying what I should've said last year. At letting you think I didn't care when I've thought about you every day since."

Her lips part just slightly, like she's ready to interrupt, but I don't let her. Not this time.

"I'm good at screwing things up," I say, softer now, "but I'm really damn good at learning from my mistakes."

She crosses her arms—not defensive, just needing something to do with her hands it appears. "What are you saying, Liam?"

My jaw tightens. "Like I told you at the hospital. I was scared."

She raises an eyebrow. "Of me?"

"Of how much I wanted you. Of what it would mean if I let myself really go there." I let a breath out slowly, steadying myself. "But I'm not scared now."

A long beat passes between us. I can practically hear her thinking, weighing the words, the timing, the risk.

She tilts her head. "Still not subtle."

I grin. "I'll work on it."

Juniper bites her lip, clearly trying to hold back a smile. "So, dragging me out of a chair, huh?"

"Still on the table."

Her laugh escapes, soft and reluctant, but it's real. And in that sound, in the way she's still here—not running, not brushing me off—I feel the tension between us shift.

"We should go inside."

I nod and follow her up the staircase.

Inside her flat, we slip off our shoes and hang up our coats.

Trying to calm down, I take a moment in the bathroom to wash up and brush my teeth.

When I enter her room, Juniper's sitting on the edge of her bed, still in that deep burgundy dress that's been tormenting me all night. Her legs are crossed, hands braced behind her, watching me like she's not sure what move I'll make next, or if she wants to make the next move herself.

I stand in the doorway for a moment, drinking her in while her eyes stay locked on mine.

"Hey," I say quietly.

"Hey."

I move toward her, slow and steady. "If you want me on the couch—"

"No," she says immediately, voice firm. "I want you here."

That's all the invitation I need.

I climb onto the bed, pushing her backwards until she's pinned beneath me, my hands braced on either side of her head.

The moment my pelvis drops against hers, we both groan. It feels so right to have her under me. To enjoy the feel of her soft curves reaching up to meet me without an ounce of guilt. I'm so fucking captivated by her, tonight only made it more apparent.

I brush a loose hair off her forehead, letting my fingers continue to trace over the shell of her ear then her jaw.

"I didn't like seeing you and Beck flirting."

"Is that what we were doing?" She lifts her brows, a small laugh escaping her throat. "It felt like a one man show I just happened to be sitting next to."

"I don't think you understand how possessive I can be,"

I murmur, dipping my head closer, letting my fingers lightly squeeze at the base of her neck.

"So show me," she says, voice low and daring.

I pause, just long enough for her to read the hunger in my eyes, then I release her. Stepping back, until I'm standing again and I can see her fully, I curl my finger. "Come here."

She sits up, taking my hands when I offer them. No hesitation, just heat and trust and the same ache I've been feeling since the moment I saw her again.

I guide her over to the full-length mirror by her closet and position her in front of me.

"Ask me to help you with your zipper."

Her eyes meet mine in the mirror. She knows this scene. It's chapter thirteen of her annotated book that I've been reading.

Turning her head to speak over her shoulder, she looks up at me from under her long lashes. "Will you unzip me?"

My head bows to examine the zipper. Then, with deft fingers, I easily glide it down her back.

"Thanks," she says, holding the now loosened dress up to her chest.

"You're welcome."

I trace the outline of the tattoo behind her ear. It's an open book with three hearts floating off the pages.

The sight of her ink has me already breaking character.

"Is this new?" I ask, combing her hair to the other side to get a better view.

"I got it when I opened Blush & Binding. To commemorate the event."

"I like it." I brush my thumb over the tattoo, and she shivers.

"Are you cold?"

She shakes her head. "Quite the opposite."

"Hmm." With my nose buried in her hair, my lips press against the sensitive skin of her neck. I focus on returning to the scene we're role playing. The one where two quarreling roommates become lovers. "I liked us tonight. It was almost as if you could stand me."

"Liam." She sighs.

Fuck. I love hearing my name on her lips.

I turn my head, meeting her eyes in the mirror.

"What am I going to do with you, Firefly?"

The scene is a loose interpretation because I can't not talk to her like she's mine.

"Touch me."

On cue, she releases the top of her dress and it pools at her feet.

The visual of Juniper standing in front of the mirror in her bra, lacy thong and sheer tights is electrifying. My fingers have been inside her, yet I've never *seen* her. Not like this. Not fully exposed.

I don't regret what happened at the hospital today—not for a second—but I'm dying to see all of her now, in the warm light of her bedroom, where nothing about this feels rushed or hidden.

She shifts slightly, her gaze flicking between our reflections and mine over her shoulder.

"This isn't quite the same as the book," she whispers. "She didn't have a bra on. Or tights. Because it wasn't winter."

"That's an easy fix."

She reaches for the waistband of her tights, but I stop her by closing my hand gently over hers. "Let me do it."

A tiny gasp escapes her lips. It's barely a sound, but it makes my cock strain against the zipper of my pants.

This isn't about me, though.

I kneel behind her, my fingers curling inside the waistband. "You annotated this scene with three stars and a flame," I say against her skin. "But I think you undersold it."

She laughs softly, breath hitching as I slowly, deliberately, pull the tights and her thong down her legs, dragging them over her hips, her thighs, and finally her knees. My mouth follows the trail, kissing her inner thigh, then the back of her knee.

She's trembling now—not from nerves, but anticipation.

"I didn't realize you read the annotations," she whispers.

"I've read every one," I say, lips brushing her skin. "Especially the ones about what you'd want someone to do to you."

I rise behind her again, fingers gliding up her sides, feeling the goosebumps rise beneath my palms. I unclasp her bra, and she lets it fall down her arms and onto the floor.

In the mirror, our eyes meet.

Juniper is stunningly naked while I'm fully clothed, and I love seeing her like this. The fact that she's letting me do this with her is everything.

The mirror is nice, but glancing down over her shoulder I get an overhead view of her full breasts and the way her rosy nipples are pinched so fucking tight.

God, she's perfect and I'm going to take my time proving to her what she means to me.

I bend, letting my mouth trail kisses across the slope of her shoulder, against the curve of her spine. Her breath catches when I brush my thumbs beneath the swell of her breasts, teasing slowly before my hands cup her fully.

"Liam," she breathes, her voice wrecked and wanting as she arches into my hands.

"Fuck, Firefly. Look how beautiful you are." I thumb over one tight nipple, then the other. "I've wanted to touch you like this for so long."

"Please, Liam. I need more."

"That's right. You do."

I take a step back, but one hand on the small of her back keeps her upright.

"What are you—"

I walk across the room to pull the small fabric reading chair from the corner, and position it in front of the mirror.

Her eyes widen. Did she think I wasn't going to play this out exactly how it was written? That I wouldn't give her everything she highlighted and noted in the margins of the book? Give her everything she asked for? And even things she didn't, but I know she wants?

I push my sleeves up, then take a seat.

"Come here."

She walks over to me, and I pull her into my lap with her back tucked against my chest.

"You feel that?" I murmur against the shell of her ear, our eyes locked in the mirror. "This is what you do to me, Firefly."

My cock is throbbing beneath her, trapped against the confines of my pants, but this isn't about me. Not yet.

I rub my palms along the arms of the chair, warming them before I make contact with her skin. Even so, her breath hitches when I run my warm palms up her thighs, slow and deliberate.

"You don't get to look away," I whisper in her ear. "This is what you wanted, isn't it? Someone who sees you. All of you."

I drag my hands up her stomach, slow and steady, until I'm cupping her breasts, teasing my thumbs over her nipples. Her body arches back into me like she can't help it.

"Spread your legs, Firefly. Show me how wet you are for me."

She complies and we both moan at the sight of her slick cunt reflected in the mirror.

"You look so fucking good like this. Open. Waiting. Desperate."

She shudders, biting her lip. Her eyes meet mine in the mirror—wide and hungry—and I can feel it in every inch of her...she's never been looked at like this. Worshipped like this.

My hand trails lower, over her belly, then teases between her thighs. She gasps.

"Keep your eyes on me," I say. "I want you to watch while I make this fantasy real. I want you to see how much I enjoy playing with your sweet little cunt. And how fucking wet you get."

She nods, barely holding herself together, and when my fingers slip inside her, I feel just how ready she is for me. Wet. Warm. Already shaking.

And still watching.

"You're not going to come until I say so."

She whimpers.

When I add a second finger, her walls tighten around me.

"You'll hold on...because you trust me."

Her eyes flutter closed, and I slow my touch immediately.

"Uh-uh, open your eyes, Firefly. You're not going to miss this."

She blinks at the mirror again, lips parted, eyes glassy with want.

"That's it," I whisper. "Watch your slick cunt swallow my fingers."

I thrust inside again, and we both watch as she takes my fingers deep inside her.

*Fuck.*

It's almost too much. The sight of her, flushed and writhing in my lap. Her slick warmth coating my fingers.

"Look in the mirror, Juniper," I murmur, my mouth brushing her ear as I slip my hand between her thighs again. "That wrecked girl is all mine."

She shudders, her breath stuttering as I slide my fingers back inside her, slow but deep enough to make her hips twitch.

"Your mouth, your cunt—they're mine to ruin," I growl against her neck, kissing the skin just below her ear. "Say it."

She moans, half defiance, half surrender. "Yours."

"Good girl. Now watch while I make you prove it."

She sighs, hips grinding down onto my hand, and I can feel how close she is. How her walls flutter around my fingers, trying to pull me deeper.

I press my mouth to her shoulder, teeth grazing her skin as I say, "Look at you, Firefly. So fucking pretty spreading those legs for my fingers."

I thrust them deeper, slow and filthy, watching her eyes flutter as she tries to keep them open.

"Watch how wet you get for me. Look how well your cunt grips me—fuck, you're so tight. Next time it won't be my fingers. It'll be my cock stretching you open while you watch yourself drip all over me."

She moans, and I pump harder, dragging my thumb over her clit. Giving her the pressure there that she needs.

"I want you to see how wrecked you look when you come for me. You're mine to ruin—every inch of you."

Her breath catches, and her thighs tremble. She's so close.

"Now let go, baby," I whisper. "Be a good girl and come for me."

I circle her clit and with one more thrust and curl of my fingers, she shatters. Crying out my name as her body writhes in my lap, her reflection a beautiful, fucked-out masterpiece in the mirror.

# JUNIPER

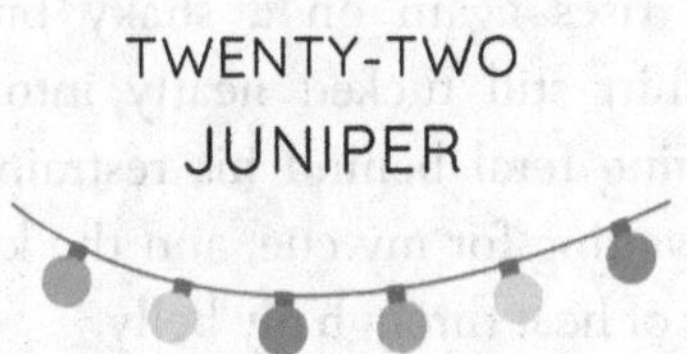

MY BODY IS warm and buzzing, my skin flushed, my heartbeat erratic—but it's not just from what he did to me. How hard I came around his fingers.

It's from how he looked at me while he did it.

Like I was art. Like I was his.

The mirror doesn't lie. I see the red flush on my chest, the way my nipples are still tight from being watched so intensely. I see the damp shine between my thighs, proof of how completely he unraveled me with just his hands and that voice. The dirty talk was next level. I think it might have been filthier than the scene in the book.

And I see him, still behind me, his broad chest rising beneath his shirt, eyes dark and fixed on mine like he's not done. Like he's barely gotten started.

I've never felt this exposed. Not just physically, but emotionally. Like he's peeled back every layer of my defenses, and all that's left is want. Need. A reckless kind of craving.

I should be overwhelmed. But I'm not. Because Liam's

gaze hasn't wavered—not once. He's not smirking. He's not smug. He's reverent.

I don't think anyone's ever looked at me like this. Like I'm both the fire and the fuel.

My chest rises again on a shaky breath. He's still dressed, his shirt still tucked neatly into his pants, but there's something feral behind his restraint. He's holding back for me, waiting for my cue, and the knowledge sends another flicker of heat through my belly.

He worshipped me without undressing himself.

And I want to worship him right back.

"You want to keep going?" he asks, voice husky as his lips brush over my shoulder.

I can hear the need in his voice. And I can still feel the painfully hard length of him beneath my ass.

"Yes," I say. No hesitation.

Because in this moment, there's no fear left. No embarrassment or panic at the thought of showing Liam everything I am. There's only moving forward with whatever this is between us. Even if it only lasts for tonight or for the week, I want it.

"Good," he says, brushing his thumb across my bottom lip before he captures my mouth with his own. "Then get on the bed."

I move off his lap and sit at the edge of the bed.

Liam stands then steps in front of me, watching me. His chest rises slowly, his eyes burning like he's memorizing me all over again—my parted lips, my bare breasts, the trust I'm offering him without a single word.

He starts by pulling off his sweater and setting it on the chair behind him. Then, he reaches for the buttons on his shirt, working them one by one, slow and deliberate. No rush. No performance. Just his eyes on mine while the fabric parts, revealing the golden skin of his chest, the sharp cut of his abs, and that trail of hair that disappears below his waistband.

When the shirt finally slips off his shoulders, he tosses it aside. His fingers go to his belt next, the sound of the leather sliding through the loops making my stomach flip. The clink of the buckle. The soft rasp of his zipper. It all feels louder with my heartbeat in my ears.

He watches me the whole time. Like he wants me to see every inch he's going to give me.

When he steps out of his pants, I get my first look at how hard he is for me, straining against the fabric of his briefs.

He doesn't say a word as he hooks his thumbs in the waistband and slides them down.

His cock springs free and I swear I lose my ability to breathe for a full five seconds.

"Oh," I blurt, before I can stop myself. "Well. That's… ambitious."

His mouth curves into a knowing grin, cocky and lethal. "Ambitious?"

I lick my lips, my eyes still glued to him. "I mean, I've read about this kind of confidence, but I didn't think it actually existed in the wild."

Liam laughs—low, sinful, completely unbothered—and strokes a hand down his length like he's doing it just to mess with me. "You going to be okay?"

"Physically? Emotionally? Spiritually?" I raise a brow. "Unclear. But I'm willing to find out."

That earns me a groan as he steps closer and strokes a knuckle along my jaw. "You're the one sitting there like a feast, Firefly. I'm just trying to keep up."

I reach for him then, wrapping my hand around him for

the first time, and his breath hitches. He's hot and hard in my grip, and my own pulse ricochets at the weight and heat of him.

"Fuck," he groans. "I love your hands on me."

I stroke him harder and soon there's precum leaking from his tip. I reach forward to lick it, but Liam has other plans.

"Lie back. Head over the edge of the bed."

Without a second thought, I scoot back to lie across the bed, letting my head hang just over the edge like I've imagined in more than one late-night fantasy. My hair spills over, nearly brushing the floor, while my chest rises with each breath, and I wait.

He moves to the edge of the bed, and the sight of him upside down makes my pulse throb everywhere at once.

"Now open that perfect mouth for me, Firefly," he says softly, but there's nothing soft about his gaze. "I want you to take me just like this. I want to see your lips stretched so fucking tight around me."

I open for him. Greedy, aching, desperate for the way he's looking at me—like I'm the only thing that's ever satisfied him, yet I haven't even started.

My tongue slips out to swirl the head of his cock, finally getting a taste of him.

As I wrap my lips around him and begin to move, his hands brace on either side of my ribs, keeping me still beneath him, and he groans like he's coming undone. But I can feel the control simmering in him—tight, electric, coiled.

He bends over me and drops a kiss to my belly. Loving the sensation of his mouth there, my hips rock upward.

The angle changes and I take him farther into my mouth.

I swirl my tongue around the head of his cock, feeling a shiver ripple through him as I tighten my grip around his base. His fingers flex at my hips, and I can tell he's barely holding on.

But then, without warning, he leans forward. One hand slides up my thigh, spreading me open again, and the next thing I know, his mouth is on me.

His tongue sweeps up my center, hot and slow. The sensation liquefies me. For a moment, I lose my rhythm, my hand faltering on his shaft as a moan catches in my throat.

He doesn't let up.

One hand curls around my thigh, anchoring me, while the other spreads across my lower belly, keeping me perfectly tilted to him. I can't see him from this angle, but I feel everything. Every breath. Every flick of his tongue. Every soft groan that vibrates straight through my core.

Then he pulls back just enough to speak, his voice low and rough against my skin.

"Fuck, Firefly," he mutters, kissing the inside of my thigh. "You taste like sugar and sin."

I have no words. All I can think is I wonder how we look right now? My head hanging off the bed with his cock down my throat while he licks between my legs.

The sensation of him licking me while I have him in my mouth is a sensory overload I never could've prepared for. A sharp bolt of pleasure zips through me, and I moan, the vibration pulling a curse from deep in his chest.

"That feel good, Firefly?"

I hum a yes, mouth full, and he chuckles darkly before diving back in. It's messy and maddening and so utterly him—always pushing, always wrecking me in the best way.

And all I can think, as he worships me from between

my legs while I do the same for him, is how completely I've unraveled in his hands.

And how I never want this—him—to stop.

I suck him deeper in response, needing something to ground me, to keep me tethered through the way he's absolutely wrecking me with his mouth.

His groan vibrates against me again. "You're addictive."

He presses two fingers inside me, and I gasp, my thighs beginning to tremble. "Oh my god…"

"Come for me," he growls, more command than plea. "I want every drop of it, baby."

And then he sucks my clit, firm and steady, and it detonates something inside me. I come hard, thighs shaking, my cry choked around his cock as I fall apart against his mouth.

He growls in satisfaction, licking me through it, like he's trying to memorize the way I taste, the way I sound, the way I fall to pieces just for him.

"You're mine," he whispers, like a vow only the two of us will ever hear.

When he pulls back, he drags one last, slow kiss over my sensitive flesh, like he can't stand to leave me. Then he stands, towering over me again.

My eyes lift, catching the sight of him—his lips and jaw slick with me, eyes dark, chest heaving like he's the one who just came undone.

The sight punches another needy sound out of me.

I gasp around him, the sound muffled by his cock nudging past my lips again. He grips my hair, just tight enough to hold me in place as he rocks his hips forward, groaning low.

"Look at you," he rasps, voice wrecked. "Look at you taking me so fucking pretty—your taste still on my tongue—fuck—"

He thrusts deeper, careful but hungry, and my lashes flutter as I swirl my tongue around him, savoring the salt and heat.

I feel him tremble, feel the last thread of his control start to slip.

His hips stutter. His grip tightens.

"I'm gonna—shit, I'm—"

He comes with a low growl of my name, spilling into my mouth as I hold him steady, coaxing every last tremble out of him. He doesn't pull away until he's breathless and dazed, eyes wide and reverent as he looks down at me like I've just rewritten every rule he ever knew.

"Holy hell," he murmurs, dropping to his knees to kiss me, deep and messy and grateful.

When we finally come up for air, we're tangled together in the center of my bed, limbs loose and bodies humming.

And for a moment, there's nothing in the world except the sound of our breathing, and the realization that we've just crossed a line we can't uncross.

I turn, then lift my head to see his face. He's already watching me like he's trying to memorize every freckle, every eyelash, every piece of me he didn't get to touch yet.

He lifts a hand, brushing his knuckles over my cheek, his thumb tracing the corner of my mouth like he's remembering himself there.

"You okay?" he murmurs, voice hoarse but so gentle it makes my chest ache.

"Yeah." My lips curve, a soft, shy smile I can't quite stop. "Are you?"

"Yeah, but I'm never going to be the same." He huffs a laugh, warm and low, and drops a kiss to my forehead. "Honestly, you wrecked me, Firefly."

Heat floods my cheeks. I bury my face in the curve of

his neck, inhaling the scent of us together. I playfully nudge him with my knee. "You deserved it."

"Hmm." He dips his head to kiss my nose, then my cheek, then the corner of my mouth. Each one slower than the last.

His lips linger at my temple, but when he pulls back, his eyes sweep down my body and the warmth in them shifts, a flicker of care beneath the haze of satisfaction.

"Hey," he murmurs, voice still low and a little rough. "Lie back for me a sec."

I blink, confused but pliant as he shifts away, reaching for the box of tissues on my nightstand.

"You don't—" I start, but he cuts me off with a look that's so tender it makes my chest ache.

"Shh, Firefly. Let me take care of you."

I settle back against the pillows, watching him as he gently parts my thighs, cleaning me up with slow, careful strokes that make my cheeks flush all over again. It's not sexual, not exactly, but the way he does it, so gentle and focused, feels more intimate than anything that came before.

When he's done, he presses a soft kiss to my inner thigh, then looks up at me with that boyish, crooked grin.

"All good?" he asks, voice quiet.

"Yeah," I breathe, warmth blooming in my chest so big it almost hurts. "Thank you."

He tosses the tissues, then crawls back up beside me, tucking me close like he can't stand the thought of even an inch between us.

He kisses my forehead, the bridge of my nose, the corner of my mouth. It's slow and unhurried. Like he has nowhere else to be.

"Stay here tonight?" I whisper, my words muffled against his skin.

"Try and get rid of me," he says, so soft and certain it twists something deep in my chest.

He curls his hand at my hip, his other brushing lazy circles on my back. I hum, sleep already pulling at the edges of me.

"I really like this," I mumble, half-asleep now, the words slipping out before I can swallow them down.

He kisses my hair, his breath warm at my temple. "Me, too, Firefly. Me, too."

And when his arms tighten around me, holding me safe and steady, I know that I can let myself believe it.

I drift off to sleep with his heartbeat beneath my ear and his name warm on my lips.

I LEAVE Juniper tangled in the sheets, soft breaths drifting over her pillow, a pink flush still lingering on her skin as proof I didn't dream any of it.

The kitchen smells like cinnamon spice from that little candle she likes to burn. Beck is perched on the counter, drinking straight from the orange juice carton and wearing my hoodie like he owns the place.

"You ever heard of a glass?" I mutter, grabbing a mug for coffee. "You're like a wild animal sometimes."

He shrugs, his eyes flicking to the faint bite mark on my collarbone from when Juniper lost her mind last night. Or maybe it was early this morning? Hard to say, since the night blurred between sleep-warm cuddling and those raw moments under the covers when I dropped below the sheets to taste her again. I couldn't get enough of her skin or that sweet little sound she makes when she falls apart for me.

"I could say the same thing about you. You've got bite marks on your collarbone, yet you haven't even asked the girl out on a proper date."

I pause, coffee mid-pour. "What?"

"A date, Liam." He grins, all fake innocence. "You know, hot cider, holding hands, romantic gestures that women love. The stuff normal people do before they...well —" he gestures vaguely at my neck,"—that."

I've been wrapped up in helping Juniper at her store and getting the wine bar ready. I've only been playing defense. Reacting to the moments instead of creating them.

I'm an idiot and Beck is, unfortunately, here to witness it.

I pinch the bridge of my nose, already regretting letting him in the door. "Shit."

Beck barks out a laugh. "You didn't, did you? You've been so busy trying to make amends for last year, you forgot to start with the basics. Courtship. Romance. A date."

Before I can tell him to shut up, the bedroom door creaks open, and a moment later Juniper appears in nothing but my shirt. Her hair is a mess, sleep still in her eyes. She's the prettiest damn thing I've ever seen.

"Good morning." She moves slowly toward the coffee machine. "Who forgot what?"

Beck lifts his juice like a toast. "Your boy here forgot to actually ask you out."

Juniper's brows shoot up, her mouth tugging into an amused little smile. "Oh, really?"

I drag a hand through my hair. "I was going to—"

Beck cuts in. "When? After you two burn through her mattress?"

"Beck—" I grit out, but Juniper's laughing now, hiding it behind her hand.

Juniper steps closer, tilting her head at me. "So? What did you have in mind?"

Good thing I'm used to thinking on my feet.

I set my mug down and close the space between us,

ignoring Beck's smug grin behind me. "Will you come with me to the Holiday Market today? Just us," I toss over my shoulder in case Beck is looking to be a third wheel. "I'll buy you hot cocoa and funnel cake, then look at all the crafts. Hell, I'll win you a pinecone ornament or whatever prize they offer at these things. An actual date. Very official."

Her smile goes soft; all sleep and sweet and amused. "Yeah. That sounds nice."

Behind us, Beck claps. He's way too pleased with himself. "Thank god. Maybe now I can survive this week without needing earplugs."

I flip him off without looking back, staying focused on the way Juniper's cheeks flush when I brush a kiss to her temple.

"I'm going to hold you to that pinecone ornament," she says, her mouth teasing into a smirk as she turns to pour her coffee.

"I'll win you a whole fucking tree."

We're only ten minutes into the Holiday Market and Juniper's already dragged me to three different booths, handed me two sample cups of steaming cider, and squealed over a basket of handmade ornaments shaped like tiny snow boots.

It's cold enough for our breath to fog between us. Lights twinkle from every booth and garland is strung across the stalls like the whole town conspired to look like a goddamn Christmas card.

I've been to Christmas markets before—New York, London, LA—slick city versions with overpriced mulled wine and crowds that make you want to throat punch someone. But here? Here it's families, kids with sticky marsh-mallow fingers, an old man with a beard like Santa passing out peppermint bark samples, and Juniper—radiant in her knitted beanie and mittens, eyes wide at every stand like she's five seconds from adopting an entire crate of home-made candles.

She pulls me toward a stall selling gingerbread cookies shaped like snowflakes. "Liam, look!" She holds up one with this triumphant grin like she just discovered gold. "They're too pretty to eat."

"But you're going to sample them anyway, right?" I hand over cash for the cookies while Juniper beams up at me with a flirty smile.

I lean closer, brushing my hand over the small of her back, fighting the stupid urge to buy every last cookie just to keep that look on her face. "You're getting crumbs all over your mittens, Firefly."

She sticks her tongue out at me and takes a delicate bite anyway, a sprinkle falling onto her scarf. She giggles, then flicks the crumb at my chest.

I should feel ridiculous here, holding a half-finished cider in one hand and a bag of overpriced fudge in the other, but I don't. I feel steady. Like I could do this a thousand times. Stand in the cold, carry her shopping bags, watch her get excited about things that feel small and big all at once.

She loops her arm through mine, tugging me toward another stall. This one is selling carved wooden signs that say things like *Home Sweet Home* and *Merry & Bright*.

"See anything you like?" she teases, brushing her hip into mine.

"Yeah," I say, my voice low so only she hears. "I do."

She rolls her eyes, but her cheeks flush pinker than the cold can take credit for.

And I swear—for a split second—this place, this market, this moment, feels like a preview of something I didn't know I could have until now.

Not just the small-town life. Not just the pine-scented candles and cider, twinkle lights, and holiday traditions.

But her. In it.

Every holiday market. Every snowy December. Every soft smile and gingerbread crumb and mittened hand tugging me through a crowd.

*Her.*

She turns, catches me staring, and raises a brow. "What?"

"Nothing," I say, leaning down to brush a kiss to her temple. "Just thinking I'm glad Beck ran his mouth this morning."

She smiles. "Me, too."

We continue working our way through the maze of stalls until we reach the far end of the market where a giant snow castle sits under a halo of string lights. Kids are climbing through tunnels carved in the walls, parents are snapping photos. A volunteer at the entrance calls out, "Watch your head! It's slippery in there!" but Juniper just looks at me with that spark in her eyes and I already know we're going in.

"Five minutes. Humor me."

Five minutes? She doesn't even realize she's got me forever.

It's quiet inside—muffled from the outside noise, like the world shrank down to just her breath in the cold and my pulse hammering in my ears.

She turns, cheeks pink, breath fogging the air between us. "Tell me this isn't amazing."

"It's amazing," I say, but I'm not looking at the walls. I'm looking at her—lips parted, eyes bright, every inch of her soft and bundled up except for that wicked glint that says she's thinking things she probably shouldn't in a snow fort full of children's laughter echoing outside.

She steps closer, pressing her palms to my chest, voice low. "You're looking at me weird."

I lean down, brushing my nose over hers. "You're trouble, you know that?"

"Why?" she breathes, fingers fisting in my coat.

"Because you keep looking at me like that."

She tips her chin up, grin turning sly. "Like what?"

"Like you want me to forget I'm supposed to be a gentleman," I murmur, my lips ghosting over her jaw, my hands bracing her hips.

She hums, shifting closer until my back hits an icy wall and she's pressed up against me, warm and soft under all her winter layers. "Maybe I do."

"Juniper—" I start, but she cuts me off with a kiss that's all teeth and tongue, hungry and impatient in a way that makes my restraint snap like a twig under snow.

I groan, catching her bottom lip between my teeth, my hands sliding down to cup her ass through her thick coat. She makes a soft sound—half giggle, half gasp—and I swear, if we weren't standing in a snow castle I'd have her under me in seconds.

She pulls back just enough to whisper, "What are you going to do about it?"

I let out a low laugh, voice dark against her ear. "First? I'm going to get you out of here before you push me past my limit."

She shivers, but it's not from the cold. Then, she tips her hips forward, testing me.

I drop my mouth to her neck, letting my breath tickle her skin. "And when we're alone..." My teeth graze her earlobe. "I'm going to spread you out on that cozy bed of yours and taste every inch of you until you're begging me to let you come."

She whimpers. I catch the sound with another kiss, deep and filthy and nothing like a small-town holiday moment.

Outside, a kid squeals and someone laughs, the reminder that we're not alone forcing me to pull back before I ruin her mittened hands on the frozen wall behind me.

She's breathless, wide-eyed, lips swollen from my mouth. "So..." she pants, grin curling wicked at the edges. "Hot chocolate next?"

I huff out a laugh, pressing my forehead to hers. "God, Firefly. Yeah. Hot chocolate. Then I'm taking you home and wrecking every sweet thought you've ever had about snow castles."

She laughs, and it's the sound of pure mischief, before she pulls me back through the tunnel, her small hand warm in mine.

And I follow. Willingly. Like I'd follow her anywhere.

## TWENTY-FOUR
## JUNIPER

THIS IS A DISASTER. A mess. A complete, flaming dumpster fire.

Not my event. The event is flawless. *I'm* the mess.

I've been planning the hell out of Books & Bubbly for over two months. Every detail, every local vendor, every perfect sparkling pour of prosecco. Pinterest-level cozy, small-town holiday magic. Except I didn't account for one tiny problem...Liam.

Liam with his cozy sweaters and crooked smile and just enough scruff on his face to be fucking delectable. And that's just the way he looks. Never mind the fun we have together. Laughing and people watching. Sampling hot cocoa with just enough peppermint schnapps to make our bellies warm and our limbs tingly. Buying scented holiday soaps so we could sample them in the shower together. That was right after he pressed me to the tile and made me come with his mouth.

And yet...we still haven't had sex. My body is practically vibrating with want.

I want him. Badly. Desperately. Every inch of me wants

to throw caution to the wind, to give in to what I know would be explosive and magnificent.

But I can't. Not yet. Because if I do—if I let him in fully, if we cross that line—the denial ends. And when the denial ends, there's no going back. I'd fall, head over heels, and the idea of him leaving afterward? I might never recover. My heart would be a pile of glittering wreckage on the floor of this bookstore.

So instead, I'm hiding behind the register, rearranging bookmarks for the hundredth time, while my brain rewinds *Liam Hargrove: Greatest Hits* on loop. My hands are busy. My mind? Not so much.

I should be focused on the author signing line that's wrapped halfway around the store, the champagne flutes clinking on every table, the raffle tickets. Instead, I'm hyper-aware of him. The way he smiles at Mrs. Bryan, the local librarian, like he's been a regular here for years. The way he remembers how to refill the drink cooler without asking, or the way he looks at me when he thinks I'm not paying attention.

And worst of all?

I can still feel him. Last night's heat, lingering just beneath my skin, the memory of his hands, his mouth, the way he made me come so completely...it's right there, threatening to unravel me.

Part of me hoped the last few nights with him would be enough. Enough to take the edge off. But it only sharpened it. Made the craving worse. Made me painfully aware of how much I'm holding back.

I think about the version of me last year that asked Liam to be my first and damn it, I was so naïve. I had no idea what it would be like to have that man's attention and now, I can't imagine what it would be like not to.

It doesn't help that he's across the room right now in a soft black sweater that makes my palms itch. Sleeves pushed up just enough to show off those forearms that has my brain turning to mush.

"We're out of prosecco."

I blink away Liam and focus on what Charlotte is telling me.

"You're kidding."

She makes a face. "Unfortunately, no. But the good news is the event is a huge success."

"Yeah, that's great but we still have an hour left and some people haven't even used their drink tickets."

"Want me to run to the store?"

Before I can answer Charlotte, a low rumble of a voice cuts in—his voice.

"I've got it covered."

I swear my heart does a somersault so dramatic it should get a standing ovation.

I look up and find Liam still leaning against the shelf, arms crossed, sleeves shoved up just so, watching me like he knows exactly how scrambled my brain is right now—and exactly why.

"You've got what covered?" I ask, trying to keep my voice level. Trying not to think about how that stupid vein on his forearm looks when he pours champagne. Or other, dirtier things.

He pushes off the shelf and strolls closer, just enough that I catch a whiff of the sweet vanilla scent drifting from the big tray of sugar cookies on the checkout counter. It mixes with his cologne and does ridiculous things to my focus. "More prosecco. I'll handle it."

"You have prosecco just lying around?" Charlotte asks, her brow lifting like she's clocking something I'm missing.

Liam's smile is all innocence, which is funny, because there's not a single innocent thing about that man. He shrugs one shoulder, easy and unbothered. "Let's just say I know where to find a bottle or two. Don't worry about it, I'll be right back."

"Liam—" I start, because I want to ask. Where? How? But he's already dropping a quick kiss on my temple—so casual, so unfair—and murmuring just for me, "Focus on your party, Firefly. I've got you."

And just like that, he's out the door into the cold, leaving me blinking at the bell above the entrance.

Charlotte nudges me with her elbow. "So, he just happens to have prosecco?"

I shove a stack of bookmarks at her to distract her suspicious grin. "Just go pass these out."

She laughs but lets it drop. Thank god.

I watch through the frosted window as Liam starts down the sidewalk, his broad shoulders disappearing around the corner.

The man drives me insane in the best way possible. And apparently, he's also my emergency prosecco supplier now.

I press a hand to my still-warm cheek, trying to pull myself together. One crisis averted. One infuriating, irresistible distraction multiplied.

And the worst part?

I think I love every second of it.

The last guest leaves with a satisfied sigh and a tote bag of signed books tucked under her arm. When the door swings shut behind her, the little bell above it jingles one final time before the shop settles into a hush.

Before I even glance up, I quickly open my laptop and type out a message to *PourChoices*.

*JuniReads*: The event was a success! We actually needed more prosecco at the end, but my once-annoying houseguest turned prosecco supplier saved the day.

I hit send and almost immediately, a reply pops up.

*PourChoices*: Knew it would be a success. And I have to say your houseguest seems to have been more helpful than expected. Glad he's on your team.

I smirk at the screen, feeling a flicker of warmth at his words, and close the laptop. Somehow, it's oddly satisfying to share the event triumph with him, even anonymously.

I glance up and freeze. Liam is leaning against a bookshelf across the store, phone in hand, sleeves pushed to his elbows, watching me with that look that turns my insides to syrup. My chest tightens. He doesn't move when I flick off the twinkle lights or start stacking stray champagne flutes by the register. He just tracks me, like he's memorizing every place my hands touch.

After the prosecco crisis was averted, Liam had made an exhausted Charlotte leave early, insisting he'd help me finish the event.

"You really didn't have to help," I say, tossing stray napkins into the trash.

"I know," he says, one corner of his mouth lifting. "But I like watching you work."

I laugh, but my pulse flutters. Because I know exactly how he likes watching me.

When I reach for the extra garland still half-pinned to the side of the big window, he pushes off the shelf and crosses the room in three easy strides.

"Leave it," he murmurs, brushing a knuckle down the back of my arm. Goosebumps erupt under my sweater.

"I can finish—" I start, but his fingers circle my wrist, firm but careful.

"Juniper." My name is a command and a promise all at once. He plucks the garland from my hand and tosses it on a nearby chair. Then he nudges me backward until my hips bump the base of the big rolling ladder attached to the floor-to-ceiling shelves.

"You've been up and down this thing all night," he murmurs, eyes flicking to my mouth, then lower. "And all I could think about was you on it for me."

Heat blooms low in my belly. "The ladder?"

His eyes flash, dark and hungry. "Mmhm." He nods upward to the height of the ladder. "You, up there—spread for me."

I bite my lip, my whole body buzzing. "Someone might see—"

He smirks, hands sliding under the hem of my sweater, thumbs grazing bare skin. "Store's locked. Lights are off. It's just you and me."

And just like that, I'm gone. Every good intention I had about keeping things under control goes up in flames.

His hands settle on my waist, thumbs brushing the sliver of skin where my sweater's ridden up. He leans in, nose brushing mine. "Climb for me, Firefly."

My knees go weak, but I do it. Step by shaky step until I'm perched on the fifth rung, just high enough that his face is level with my belly. His palms glide up my thighs as he leans in and presses a slow, teasing kiss just above my knee.

His fingers slide under the hem of my skirt, then he hooks a finger in the side of my underwear, tugging the soft lace down just enough to expose me to the cool air, and his warm breath.

He drags the fabric down my thighs, slow enough to

make me shiver. My underwear falls to my ankles, and he pulls them over my heeled booties, tossing them onto the shelf behind him like they're nothing.

"Fuck, look at you," he whispers. He presses his mouth to the inside of my knee, teeth scraping just enough to make my hips jerk forward. "Already wet for me."

I grip the ladder's wooden rails tighter when his broad shoulders nudge between my thighs, spreading me open. He kisses up, up, up. A firm trail of heat that makes me squirm against the rung.

"Hold on for me, baby," he breathes against my skin. His hands slide under my thighs, palms bracing my hips as he lifts me just enough to tilt me forward. "I'm going to make a mess of you right here."

Then, his mouth is on me. Tongue stroking slow and firm. Teasing me with circles that make my vision blur.

I gasp, my back arching, forehead bumping the ladder. "Liam—"

He groans, low and filthy, like my voice alone does something to him. "Let me hear you come apart, Firefly. Every little sound."

He flicks his tongue deeper, and my knuckles go white on the ladder rail. He's relentless. Slow, then greedy, then slow again until my thighs tremble and I can't help the needy moan that slips out. He chuckles against me, the vibration sending sparks up my spine.

"You taste like heaven," he rasps, tongue flicking, then flattening to lap me open again. "And when I fuck you for real, baby—" His voice drops even lower, wicked and reverent. "You're going to soak my cock just like this."

I bite my lip, the ladder rattling under my grip as I chase the heat spiraling tight in my belly. He drags it out, building me higher, letting me hover on the edge until my hips buck forward and he groans like he loves how desperate I am for him.

A moment later, I cry out, my forehead pressed to my arm, the ladder squeaking under my shaking thighs. He doesn't stop until I'm breathless, sagging against the rungs, his mouth still tasting every last bit of me.

When he finally pulls back, his lips are slick, his eyes dark and hungry as he smirks up at me. He presses one more kiss to the inside of my thigh, then stands, crowding me against the ladder, kissing me deep so I taste myself on his tongue.

"Next time," he murmurs, his mouth brushing mine, "I'm taking you right here. Bent over these shelves. Until you forget your own damn name."

And I believe him, because the way he's looking at me? I want to forget everything that isn't him.

## TWENTY-FIVE
## LIAM

I'M STANDING IN THE JENSENS' living room, a glass of spiked eggnog in my hand, the hum of laughter and clinking glasses around me. The same twinkle lights. The same fireplace crackling under stockings stitched with names I know by heart. It's all so damn familiar.

Last year, I stood in this exact spot feeling like an outsider with a smile too polite to be real—flanked by Jasper and his family, by warmth I told myself I didn't need. I'd built my world to run on distance—homes on both coasts, a revolving door of shallow dates, and work that looked impressive but didn't mean much when I turned the lights out alone.

Then she kissed me.

Juniper Jensen. The girl who'd hovered on the edge of my orbit for nearly ten years. The one with the sharp tongue and big dreams and soft heart she guards with armor made of snark. The one who showed me in that stupid, impulsive kiss that maybe I didn't want the distance anymore.

It wrecked me. Not the kiss. The want.

How badly I wanted to say yes to her. Not because it was sex with a beautiful woman, but because I knew it would change me. She'd be under my skin in a way I'd never known, and I wouldn't be able to do anything about it.

So, I panicked. I walked away because the second her mouth touched mine, I knew. She could gut me if I let her in. And I wanted to. God, I wanted to. But I didn't know how to hold something like that. Something good.

Across the room, she's laughing at something Beck says. My traitor of a brother, who's leaning against the kitchen door with all the casual charm he's never had to earn. He's grinning wide, arms folded, eating up the attention she gives him.

She tilts her head back when she laughs, and it hits me again—this year is different. This year, I stay. I stay for every laugh, every stubborn glare, every chance she gives me to prove she's not just Jasper's sister anymore. She's mine. If she'll have me.

Beck flicks his gaze my way, clocking the look on my face. He smirks like the shithead he is and bumps her shoulder. "C'mon, Juni, you've got to admit I'd be the more fun Hargrove to keep around."

Juniper snorts, her cheeks pink from wine and warmth. "I'd rather not spend Christmas bailing you out of trouble, Beck."

I push off the mantle and close the space between us. Beck straightens just enough to brace for impact. Smart man.

"I hear you're trying to steal my girl, Beck." I hook an arm around Juniper's waist, tugging her in until her back settles against my chest.

Beck just lifts a brow, unbothered. "Can you blame me? She's way too good for you, big brother."

Juniper laughs, but when she turns back to look at me, there's a softness in her eyes.

"I don't know, Beck. Your big brother's full of surprises. I think he's got an edge over you."

Beck scoffs. "You wound me, Juni."

I dip my head, my mouth brushing her ear. "Tell him you're taken, Firefly."

She doesn't say it, but she leans her weight back into me, just enough for Beck to see exactly where her loyalty lies.

I let my lips graze the shell of her ear. "Good girl."

Beck rolls his eyes so hard I'm surprised they don't get stuck. "Disgusting. I'm getting more wine. Try not to maul her while I'm gone, yeah?"

Juniper turns just enough to shoot me a look, hazel eyes glittering under the twinkle lights. "Possessive much?"

I just grin. "You like it."

She hums, noncommittal—but when I press my palm flat against her hip, she doesn't move away.

Not this year.

Because when I leave tonight, it's with her.

And I'm making damn sure she knows: last year I ran. This year, I stay.

# TWENTY-SIX

# JUNIPER

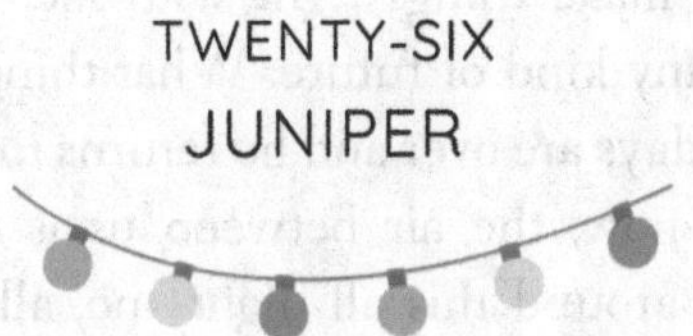

THE DOOR SHUTS BEHIND ME, and I watch Liam hang his coat in the front closet. Then, he takes mine and hangs it while I slip off my heeled boots.

We drop our keys on the table as we pass by like it's our new routine, then he follows me toward my bedroom. I guess at this point, it's our bedroom.

My family's annual holiday party had been the most fun I can remember, but this part is different. It's the first Christmas Eve that I'm not spending in my childhood home. I'm not joking with Jasper as we clean up the kitchen or cuddling on the couch beneath my favorite throw until we can't stop yawning and climb the stairs to our rooms.

I'm here in my own apartment now. With a man that has infiltrated my holiday traditions, for better or worse, and it makes me wonder where I'll be next year. If this moment with Liam will just be a snapshot in time, or will I forever associate the holiday season with Liam Hargrove and his alluring smile.

We stare at each other. Although it's late, I'm too wired to sleep.

Liam's dark eyes watch me closely.

I could get used to the way he looks at me. Like I'm something to discover and explore.

The thought is dangerous. Because even though Liam came back to make things right with me, we still haven't talked about any kind of future. What things will look like when the holidays are over and he returns to New York.

But right now, the air between us is charged. We've been dancing around this all night—no, all week—and we both know how this ends.

I stand there, back against my bedroom door, my heartbeat so loud I'm sure he can hear it. He's so close—big, warm Liam—and I know what's about to happen. What I want to happen.

He cups my face like I'm the most breakable thing he's ever held. Like he's scared I'll run if he pushes too far.

So I swallow, then force the words out before I lose my nerve. "I should tell you something."

His thumb brushes my cheekbone. "Okay."

I can't look at him. "I haven't...I mean, there hasn't been..." I let out a tiny, mortified laugh. "I'm still a virgin."

His hands still on my jaw, but his eyes flare—not with shock or judgment but something I can't quite name. Something that makes my stomach flip.

He dips his head, pressing his forehead to mine. His voice is low, rough.

"Firefly, you have no idea how fucking lucky I feel right now."

I try to pull back. "I didn't tell you so you'd celebrate it—"

His mouth cuts me off with a soft, filthy kiss with just enough tongue to make me gasp. Then, he pulls back to whisper against my lips, "I'm not celebrating that you haven't been with anyone else. I'm celebrating that I get to be the one. The only one. That I get to make this so damn good you'll never wish it was anyone else."

His words send a ripple of pleasure through me.

*So damn good you'll never wish it was anyone else.*

I can't imagine wanting anyone else the way I want Liam. Maybe that's a problem. But one for future Juniper. Because, right now, I don't want to think about what happens tomorrow, or next week when he slips from my day-to-day life again.

He tugs my sweater over my head and tosses it aside without looking. His palms find my bare waist, warm and steady, and my skin sparks under his touch.

I suck in a shaky breath, my heart thudding so hard I'm sure he can feel it through my ribs.

"You look so fucking pretty like this," he murmurs against my neck. "So damn soft for me."

"Bed?" I whisper, because my legs are already shaking.

He smiles against my collarbone, then lifts me—just like that, like I weigh nothing—and carries me the few steps to my bed. He sets me down with this gentle care that almost undoes me more than the filthy things he says.

I watch, breathless, as he straightens and peels off his shirt. His eyes never leave mine while he undoes his belt, fingers slow and deliberate, like he wants me to watch.

"You're sure?" he asks again, voice lower now, rougher. He kneels onto the bed, crowding me back against the pillows.

My answer comes out on a whisper. "More than anything."

"Good. Because once I start, Juniper..." He kisses my knee, then parts my thighs with big, confident hands. "I'm not stopping till you know you're mine."

The word *mine* curls hot in my belly.

I nod, my breath catching when he lowers himself over me, skin to skin now, heat and muscle and the rough scratch of his stubble. He kisses me again, slower this time, but deeper—and I feel him, every part of him, the weight of it, the promise.

My hands slip into his dark hair, pulling him closer, grounding myself in the press of his mouth, the slide of his palm up my thigh.

He pulls back just far enough to look at me, brushing my hair off my forehead with the backs of his knuckles. His eyes are soft but hungry, like he's memorizing everything.

"This okay?" he asks, voice hoarse.

I nod. "Better than okay."

He grins—that wicked, devastating grin—and dips his head, trailing his mouth down my throat. Lower. A soft laugh rumbles against my belly when I squirm under him, desperate for more.

"Patience, Firefly." His voice is dark silk, brushing over my skin as he kisses a path lower, lips ghosting over my ribs, my stomach. "First, I'm going to taste you. Slow. Sweet. Until you're begging to come on my cock."

My hands fly to his hair just as he reaches the edge of my thigh. He nips at the skin there, then spreads me open with a deliberate press of his thumbs. I feel like I'm on fire— the air hitting where I'm soaked for him makes me gasp.

"Look at you," he murmurs, voice thick. He blows a soft stream of air across my clit, and I jolt. "Dripping for me already."

"Liam—" I choke out.

He hums, the sound vibrating against my thigh. Then his mouth is on me. A hot, slow lick that makes my hips buck off the bed.

"Hold still, baby," he growls, pinning my hips with his strong hands. "I want to savor this."

The first flick of his tongue over my clit is torture—slow, teasing—but when he does it again, harder, I nearly sob. He laughs, dark and satisfied, then drags his tongue down to where I'm dripping, fucking me open with slow, filthy strokes that make my vision spark white.

"You taste so fucking good," he groans into me. "Could eat this sweet little cunt every damn day and never get enough."

He flicks his eyes up, catching mine—blown wide and desperate—and the look in them nearly undoes me right there. Possessive. Hungry. Like he wants to crawl inside me and never leave.

His fingers slip inside me and curl against my most sensitive spot.

"Fuck—Liam—"

He pulls back just enough to speak, mouth slick, voice like sin. "Want you to come on my tongue first. Be good for me, Firefly. Let me feel it."

He fucks me with his fingers, then seals his mouth over my clit, sucks hard—just once—and I break. My hips arch up into him, thighs trembling as I cry out, the world dissolving in a rush of heat and his name on my lips.

He keeps licking me through it, coaxing every last shudder, groaning like he's the one being wrecked. When I finally collapse against the bed, boneless and trembling, he lifts his head. His mouth is slick, his grin pure sin.

"Perfect," he rasps, kissing my thigh, my hip, my belly as he crawls up over me again. "So fucking perfect."

I can taste myself on his mouth when he kisses me, and I moan into it, half-wrecked, fully his.

"Birth control?"

"I get the shot."

His eyes flash, a dark heat mixed with something that knocks the breath out of me. He presses his forehead to mine, voice low and rough.

"Good. I want you bare. Nothing between us. Nothing keeping me from feeling every fucking inch of you."

A shiver races down my spine, but there's a flicker of worry. Not fear, just reality.

"But...have you—"

He cuts me off with a kiss that's more of a promise than anything he could say. When he pulls back, his eyes are soft but searing.

His head shakes as he huffs a rough laugh, brushing his thumb over my lips. "I haven't touched anyone since the night you kissed me. I couldn't. No one's you, Firefly."

My heart does something reckless. "Oh."

His grin is pure sin and sincerity all tangled up. "Yeah. Oh."

Then his mouth is on mine again, devouring, worshipping. And when he pulls back, his next words punch straight through my ribs.

"So, bare, baby. I want every bit of you. And I want you to feel every bit of me."

I nod. I'm already in too deep with this man. At this point, all I can do is savor every moment. Enjoy the free fall because there's no safety net. Dive in headfirst with reckless abandon and hope I'll be able to pick up the pieces later.

Then I feel him, hot and hard, nudging at my entrance. He pauses, searching my face—eyes dark, voice ragged.

"You ready, Firefly?"

My whole body answers before my mouth can. I nod, breathless, drunk on him. "Please."

His grin turns feral as he pushes forward, just enough to

make me gasp—and then he leans down, lips brushing my ear.

"Good. Now you're gonna take every inch."

I feel the first push of him, careful but insistent, and I gasp into his mouth. My fingers clutch at his shoulders, nails digging in. He pauses, forehead pressed to mine, breathing hard, voice rougher than I've ever heard it.

"God, Juniper...so fucking tight for me. You feel that?" His hips roll forward, a fraction deeper this time. I gasp again, the stretch sharp and delicious.

"Relax for me, baby," he growls, kissing the corner of my mouth, my jaw, my throat.

I do. Or at least I try.

"Fuck—look at you," he whispers, pulling back just enough to watch my face as he sinks deeper. "So pretty when you're split open for me. You know how long I've wanted this? Wanted to ruin you for every other man?"

My breath hitches at the words. Dirty. Raw. Him.

I shiver. The filth in his voice mixes with something possessive. It makes my thighs clamp tighter around his hips, drawing him closer, deeper.

"You okay?" he murmurs, but there's that wicked grin, the one that says he knows damn well I am.

"Yes—please, Liam—"

He pulls out, just enough to make me whimper, then drives back in, harder, the sound obscene in the quiet room. "Begging already," he huffs out, teeth grazing my ear. "Fuck, I love that. Love how you beg for my cock. Say it."

Heat blooms across my chest, my cheeks. My mind races but my mouth betrays me. "Want your cock—want all of it—"

"Yeah?" He bites down, gentle but possessive, right where my neck meets my shoulder. "Good girl. You're gonna take all of me. Gonna let me fill this tight little cunt so deep you'll feel me tomorrow."

I moan—I can't help it—and he laughs, low and dark. His thumb finds my clit, slow circles that make my breath hitch and my hips stutter.

"That's it, baby. Make those pretty noises. Want you so fucking loud for me." His thrusts build, harder now, deeper, the stretch pushing me to the edge of too much, but then, his mouth is on mine, catching every gasp, every broken moan.

"You're mine now," he pants against my lips, his hips grinding deeper, claiming every inch. "Mine to fuck, mine to make come, mine to keep."

My nails claw at his back, the heat coiling tight, ready to snap.

"Come for me, Firefly. Make a mess all over my cock. Let me feel how sweet this virgin pussy really is."

My orgasm crashes over me, raw and blinding. My body clamps around him so hard I feel his rhythm stutter. He groans, deep and filthy, fucking me through it until he spills inside me, buried to the hilt, forehead pressed to mine as we come apart together.

He stays there, breathing hard, lips brushing my cheek, my jaw. I feel him smile against my skin. It's a smug, satisfied curl of his mouth that makes me want to laugh and sob all at once.

"Look at you," he murmurs, voice wrecked but so damn tender. "Took it so well. My perfect girl."

# TWENTY-SEVEN
## LIAM

JUNIPER'S CURLED AGAINST ME, all warm skin and sleepy sighs. Her hair a messy halo on my chest. I drag the tip of my finger along her spine, tracing lazy circles, just looking at her. This woman has been under my skin since the second she kissed me last Christmas, and now she's under my skin in every possible way.

I can still feel her. The way she'd clung to me, breathless and brave, her mouth whispering my name when I finally pushed inside her. I'd never experienced anything like it. Never where every heartbeat felt like a promise, like I was giving something up just to gain something bigger. Us. That's what we are now.

I press my lips to the top of her head, breathing her in. God, she's wrecked me. And she doesn't even know how deep I'm in yet. I've got plans—things I want to give her, things I'm still holding close to my chest because the surprise of it is half the fun.

She shifts, half-awake, blinking up at me with that soft, hazy look that knocks every thought right out of my head.

"What?" she murmurs, voice sleepy and sweet.

"Nothing." I grin and drag my thumb across her lower lip. "Just looking."

She hums, tucking her face under my chin like she's trying to crawl inside my chest and live there.

And maybe that's what she's done. Hell, she's always been there. I just finally stopped pretending she wasn't.

She goes quiet again, breath evening out. But me? I'm wide awake, fingers on her back, brain already working out exactly how to make sure she never has to wonder if I'm staying.

And then she pushes herself up just enough to lean over the side of the bed.

"What are you doing?" I ask.

She doesn't respond. But when she leans back, she's got a small box in her hand. When she drops it on my chest, my heart actually stumbles.

It's the same box that I found in her living room earlier this week when I was helping her assemble the blind-date-with-a-book packages.

I grin. "Don't tell me you're making me unwrap something else tonight, Firefly. I'm not sure I'll survive."

She rolls her eyes but her mouth curves into that soft, secret smile I'm starting to think is reserved just for me. She presses the box into my hand. "Just open it."

I pop it open. The watch glints in the stray strip of streetlight—sleek, old-school, the brushed steel case worn smooth in places. The face is classic, but the back is what does me in—the tiny engraving near the lugs: *Tempus fugit.* A detail only another watch nerd would care about.

She'd already told me about the watch at the hospital. Admitting she'd saw it at a vintage store and thought of me. But seeing it and the engraving, and knowing it's for me from her, hits harder than I expected.

"I love it."

"Yeah?" Her voice is soft. "I love that you love it."

And damn, there's an awful lot of love circling this thing for two people who haven't said it yet.

I run my thumb over the inscription. *Tempus fugit.* Time flies. God, that hits somewhere deep.

"So let me get this straight." I tilt her chin up with my knuckle, smirking. "You carried this around all year, staring at it, and thinking about me?"

"Shut up." She shoves my shoulder but she's laughing, cheeks warm and flushed. "I wasn't pining," she lies. Badly.

"No?" I press another kiss to the corner of her mouth, slow and sweet. "So this was just, what? Casual, thoughtful hoarding?"

She swats my chest, but I catch her wrist, holding it there so she feels my heartbeat under her palm.

"You're such a pain in the ass," she says, breathless.

"Yeah?" I kiss her again, deeper now. "Well, you're the one giving sentimental vintage watches to a guy you claim you didn't miss. Makes you look a little attached, Firefly."

She tries to glare but she's smiling, soft and exasperated. "So what now?"

I flip the box shut and set it on her nightstand, then roll her beneath me in the tangle of blankets.

"Now," I say, my mouth a breath from hers, "you keep giving me your time." I nip her bottom lip just enough to make her gasp. "And tomorrow, you'll see I'm giving you mine, too."

I WAKE up warm and sore and embarrassingly content for someone who keeps insisting she's not falling in love with Liam Hargrove. But I am. Last night sealed it—like the final, soft nail in the coffin of my stubbornness.

His arm is heavy around my waist, his breath warm at the back of my neck. I shift a little, just enough to test the edge of reality, but his grip tightens like he can sense it—like if I try to slip away, he'll just pull me back under. His nose nudges behind my ear, his lips brushing my hair.

"Merry Christmas, Firefly," he murmurs, voice rough with sleep and a smug sort of tenderness that makes my chest ache.

"Merry Christmas," I sigh back, letting myself sink into him for one reckless moment.

His body is heavy and warm, like a weighted blanket that keeps my second thoughts at bay. Still, they're there— little flickers of uncertainty that bloom in the spaces between our heartbeats.

Last night was everything. Sex, yes—my first time, his hands and mouth on me, his voice whispering things I'll probably replay in my head forever. But it was more than that. The watch I'd hidden from him for months, the one I claimed Jasper had bought, when really it was mine, chosen just for Liam before I even knew how badly I'd want him to keep it. Giving it to him was like showing my whole heart, piece by piece.

He shifts behind me, his palm smoothing over my stomach, and I feel him smile into my hair.

"You're thinking too loud," he rumbles, amused and half-asleep.

I huff out a soft laugh. "Sorry."

"You say it like you mean to stop."

"It's part of my charm. Comes with the package."

He laughs, low and smug, causing his chest to rumble against my back. "Good. I'm keeping you anyway."

He says it like a promise. And the worst part is, I believe him.

After a few more minutes of cozy snuggles, he coaxes me out of bed with coffee and kisses, drapes my favorite blanket over my shoulders, and nudges me into the living room. My gingerbread advent calendar is there on the wall, catching the morning light.

It's silly, but I love that thing. I never told him how much I swooned when he started slipping little things inside. The blush hairbow. The mulled spice bag. The cherry swirl candies and the firefly brooch. He's turned it into this sweet, surprising countdown that makes my chest ache every time I see it.

He stands behind me now, close enough that I can feel the heat of him through the blanket. "Go on," he says, voice warm at my ear. "Open the last one."

I side-eye him but my heart's already fluttering. I pop open the tiny gingerbread door marked 25.

For all the small, thoughtful items that have led up to today, I'm not sure how he can top them.

Inside, I find a small brass key, tied with red ribbon. A scrap of paper underneath that reads *for us*.

I go still. For a second I can't breathe.

A key. *A key.*

*A key to what?*

Oh, god. Did he buy me a car? I don't even want a car. I can barely parallel park my Subaru.

Is it for a house? Did he buy me a house? I will absolutely pass out if he bought me a house.

Is it...*a shed*? A secret romance library shed? A wine cellar? A bunker? A tiny gingerbread cottage in the woods where he plans to keep me barefoot and stocked with romance novels until I agree to marry him?

I flick a glance at him leaning against the doorframe. A big, warm, slightly smug in the worst way smile on his face.

*Yeah, he would.* He would absolutely buy me a secret romance cottage in the woods.

"What is this?" I ask, voice way too high and squeaky.

He runs a hand through his messy hair. An adorable habit that ruins me every time. He steps closer, all heat and sweet affection. When he brushes his knuckles down my cheek, it's so gentle it makes my throat tight and my brain immediately turns to static.

"I need to show you something. Come with me?"

I glance down at my enormous T-shirt and Christmas slipper socks. I'm so unprepared for whatever life-altering thing is about to happen to me right now.

"Now?"

His grin curves, lazy and crooked. "Now."

My arms cross over my chest, covering my braless breasts and hardened nipples.

"You realize you can walk down the street naked and then just hightail it back to New York like nothing happened. I, on the other hand, live here."

His grin deepens.

"It's not far. Twenty steps, max."

*Twenty steps?* Is he going to have me leave my apartment, then walk back in?

I glance at the key again, my heart thumping. God, please don't let it be a bunker.

I convince Liam I need leggings so I don't freeze my ass off, then he patiently waits for me to put on a bra. I'm not stalling, I'm preparing myself.

After I pull on my knee-length puffer coat and stomp into my boots, Liam takes my hand like he's afraid I might change my mind halfway down the stairs. He's warm and quiet beside me, his thumb brushing over my knuckles like he can steady the small hurricane that is spinning in my chest.

Outside, Founders Street is dead quiet. It's Christmas morning at seven a.m. after all. There's nothing but soft snow under the streetlamps and the twinkle of lights hung in the trees lining the town's main business district. The only sound is our boots crunching along the sidewalk.

I glance around, half-expecting to see a giant neon sign blinking *surprise!* above one of the buildings. My brain is still racing. Is this some kind of treasure hunt? Do I have to solve a riddle? Should I be counting my steps?

But I don't have to wonder long. Liam slows us to a stop in front of the old Wild Fern storefront. The one that's under construction to become a wine bar. *PourChoices* wine bar.

My mind catches on that thought like a hook.

*PourChoices.*

The late-night forum replies that always made me feel less alone. The soft nudges to trust myself. The way *Pour-Choices* somehow knew exactly what to say to make me braver. Like he knew me. All the tiny, hidden, hopeful parts.

I turn to him, breath puffing in the cold air. *"Liam..."* There are a hundred questions in that single syllable, but only one answer I'm really asking for.

His mouth tips slightly, like he's been waiting for me to put it together.

"You're *PourChoices*." The words come out low, like saying them too loud might break the spell.

Something shifts in his expression—not guilt exactly, but something heavier. "Yeah." His voice is rough, like it costs him to say it.

"You could've just told me."

He gives a small, almost rueful smile. "I didn't know how. After that night—"

The words spark the memory before I can stop it. Christmas Eve. Sitting together on my bed, his body warm beside mine as he read through my business proposal. The way his gaze kept dropping to my mouth. That kiss—soft, then deep—until I whispered what I wanted next. How fast his warmth had vanished when he'd stood, fumbling for an excuse that wouldn't wreck me. The dull ache in my tailbone where I'd landed on the rug, matching the sharper one in my chest.

He exhales, pulling me back to the present. "I thought I'd ruined everything. But I couldn't stay away. So, I found a way to be near you, even if it meant hiding behind a stupid screen name."

The key in my palm suddenly feels like more than brass and weight—it's a map of all the quiet ways he's been here.

His thumb brushes over my knuckles, slow, tender, and impossibly intimate. My chest tightens at the simple contact.

I glance at him, the questions still unspoken, and he gives the barest shrug, eyes soft and earnest. "I wanted to be part of your world, even if I wasn't sure you'd let me."

"Even if it meant all the secrets?" I whisper, almost to myself, but sharp enough for him to hear.

He nods, letting a shiver of confession pass between us. "Every one of them. I fell for you somewhere along the way. And I had no idea how to handle that. So, I hid."

I look at the little brass key in my palm, my brain still processing his confession.

*It was him.*

He's been here all along. Not just next door, but inside every message, every push, every time I needed someone to say *you can do this.*

My eyes flick from the key to him and back. *Liam is PourChoices.*

This wine bar is his. His messages. His plan. All of it tied up in one small, shiny key.

"Go on," he says, so gentle I almost melt right there on the sidewalk.

I slide the key into the lock and turn. It sticks for half a second, like it's testing me, then clicks open.

Inside, the smell of Wild Fern is gone. No more soil and wet leaves or the faint whiff of overwatered mint.

It smells like fresh paint and oak and new beginnings. The pendant lights glow soft gold against deep green walls. Shelves line one side, already stocked with wine bottles that catch the light. The dark walnut bar gleams under soft brass fixtures. A mural stretches across the far wall—delicate vines curling and twisting up toward the ceiling like they're alive.

But it's the sign that steals my breath: *Juniper & Grove*.

My name. His name. Tied together so soft and certain it makes my heart knock against my ribs.

I run my fingers over the brass inlay of the letters to make sure they're real. They're warm under the soft lights. Warm like him, like the way he feels pressed up against my back in the morning. Steady and solid and so impossibly here.

I turn to face him. He's leaning back against the bar, watching me like he's bracing for the part where I run. Or cry. Maybe both.

"So you're staying." It slips out like a secret I've been afraid to hope for.

He nods slowly. "Yeah. If you'll have me."

I let out a laugh that's half a breath away from a sob. "Liam, your whole life is in New York. Jensen Innovations. Jasper. You can't just stay here and run a wine bar."

He pushes off the bar, stepping closer until the smell of oak and fresh paint is replaced by the smell of him—soap and winter air and something warm that's always felt like home.

"I am not giving up the company," he says, voice low and certain. "Jasper and I have been working it out for months. I'll work remote for a while, split my time. I don't need to be in Manhattan every day to keep the numbers clean."

He tips his head, eyes crinkling at the corners. "Tech CFOs work from ski resorts in Aspen, Firefly. I can run my spreadsheets from a wine bar next to your bookshop just fine."

"You planned this."

"I planned the wine bar. I hoped for you."

My heart does that stupid, reckless thing where it says yes before my brain can catch up. I'm about to kiss him again when my eye snags on a door at the back. Half hidden behind the bar wall and with a narrow staircase behind it.

I pull back just enough to point at it. "What's up there?"

He follows my line of sight, then winces. "The apartment."

I blink. "What apartment?"

He sighs, not even pretending. "Mine. It came with the lease, same as yours. I finished it a couple months ago."

My jaw drops. "You've had a place this whole time? While you were sleeping in my guest room? And then my bedroom because Beck showed up?"

He grins, smug and soft and absolutely unrepentant. "I needed a place to stay."

I gape at him. "You did not! You had an entire apartment right here."

He just stands there looking at me like I'm the best thing that's ever happened to him, completely unbothered by the fact that he's been exposed as a giant, lovesick liar.

"I didn't want the flat, Firefly." His voice drops, all soft rumble and warm hands finding my waist. "I wanted you."

My indignation fizzles the second his mouth brushes my neck—low and hot right under my ear. He knows exactly what that does to me. The traitorous part of my brain is already melting, my hands landing on his chest like I'm about to shove him away but I'm not fooling anyone.

"*Liam...*" I try to protest, but it comes out like a sigh.

His grin ghosts against my skin. "Mind if I show you how sorry I am?" His teeth graze my jaw, then he's kissing me like he's been starving for it. Deep and sweet and a little filthy just as one big hand slides under the hem of my shirt to find bare skin.

I manage a half-hearted glare. "You're—ugh, you're impossible."

He kisses the corner of my mouth, then lower. "Say yes."

I will. Of course, I will.

"Okay," I mutter, fingers curling in his shirt. "Show me upstairs then."

His laugh is low and wicked. "Gladly."

He grabs my hand, tugging me toward the back of the bar, both of us half-stumbling and giggling like teenagers sneaking out past curfew. We push through the door to the stairs—narrow, creaky, definitely not meant for what he clearly has in mind.

Halfway up, he turns and crowds me against the wall, mouth crashing onto mine, hands everywhere. I gasp into him, tugging at the back of his hair, biting his lower lip just to feel him groan against my throat.

He kisses me harder, pushing my coat off my shoulders one handed while his other arm braces against the wall like he's holding up the whole building.

When we finally reach the top, he fumbles behind me for the door handle, still kissing me, half-laughing himself now.

*Click.* The door swings open and the warm air brushes over us. Inside it's wood floors, soft rugs, the smell of new paint and fresh linens, and him, everywhere.

He backs me through the doorway, mouth still on mine, hands sliding under my oversized t-shirt again. His voice is rough against my ear. "I'm going to keep you up here for days, Firefly. I'm going—"

*Click.* Another door.

We both freeze before turning our gazes toward the sound.

Beck stands in the hallway, barefoot, hair sticking up in every direction, holding a mug like he's been living here for months.

He blinks at us once—me pressed against Liam, coat half-off, t-shirt bunched up in his fists—and lifts his mug in a lazy salute.

"Wow. Don't stop on my account."

I slap a hand over my face. Liam's forehead drops to my shoulder with a muttered curse. "Goddammit, Beck. Why are you here?"

Beck just sips his coffee—from a mug he stole from my apartment, obviously—and shrugs. "You said I could crash here last night, genius. You know, so you two could have alone time at Juniper's."

Beck points the mug at Liam like he's making a business deal. "You two figure out where you want me. Her place, your place—whatever. Just text me when it's safe to come back for my stuff." He slides past us with the world's smuggest grin, patting Liam's arm like he's congratulating him for surviving Christmas chaos. "And don't do it on my flannel blanket."

Then, he disappears down the stairs humming "Jingle Bells" like a cheerful elf.

When the door clicks behind him, the apartment falls silent again. It's just me, Liam, and the sound of my heart banging against his chest.

Liam sighs, pinches the bridge of his nose, then looks at me—that wicked, charming grin back in place.

"Firefly," he murmurs, voice already dark again as his hands slide back under my shirt, "door locked. Now."

## TWENTY-NINE
## LIAM

"DOOR LOCKED. NOW," I rumble against her neck. My nose brushes that spot just below her ear. The one that makes her knees go soft and her breath hitch in the way that drives me fucking insane.

She spins, flicks the bolt shut with a sharp click, then turns back to me. Arms crossed. Cheeks flushed. Eyes daring me to test her patience.

I take two steps and press her gently into the door she just locked. One hand by her head, the other sliding under her shirt. She's warm and soft under my palm, heartbeat pounding at my touch.

She tries for a glare, but it slips when I brush my mouth along her jaw. Her fingers twist in my shirt like she can't decide if she wants to shove me away or drag me closer.

"This is such a book boyfriend move," she says, breath hitching when my thumb strokes over her ribs, just beneath her bra. "Secret wine bar. Secret apartment. Grand gestures for days."

I grin against her skin. "Yeah? You sound like you don't hate it."

She huffs, her laugh caught somewhere in her throat. "God, you're impossible."

My heart kicks in my ribs. I can have the bar, the name, the flat next door, but none of it means shit if she doesn't want me. If she doesn't say it like she did last year when I was too much of a coward to take it.

"Say you want me anyway," I whisper against her mouth, my voice low but it cracks a little at the edge. *Please.*

She looks at me then, soft and a little wild, lips parted. I swear she can see every stupid, selfish hope running through my veins. Her hands slide up into my hair like she's trying to hold my head together so I don't fall apart.

"I always want you," she says, quiet but so certain it steals the air from my lungs.

That's all I need. I crush my mouth to hers and swallow her breath like it's mine.

Lifting her off the floor, her legs wrap around my waist easily. She fits there like she was made for me.

I carry her through the quiet flat. She's half laughing, half breathless, mumbling my name when I kick the bedroom door shut behind us. My hands grip her thighs where they're locked tight around my waist. When her eyes catch on the mirror on the closet door, she freezes for a second. Her eyes flick to it, then to me, then back again.

We look so fucking good like this.

Her hair's a mess, cheeks flushed pink from the cold outside and the way I can't keep my hands off her. Her mouth is swollen, her thighs snug around me like she never wants to let go. I don't plan on letting her.

I walk us to the bed but pause, feeling her shift in my arms. She's looking around, taking in the throw blanket identical to the one on her bed because I know how much she likes it. She cranes her neck, eyes catching on the stack of books by the lamp. Her books. The ones she annotated and I borrowed for research.

Her eyes narrow like she's going to give me shit again, but then they soften and her lips part.

Next to the books is the button she'd bought at the liquor store last year. *Spice It Up*. The one she'd snagged off the counter when I was unloading the cart. She had slipped it into my coat pocket like a secret dare. I found it two days later, back in LA, when I was already filled with regret.

She drops her legs, and I let her go. Reaching for the button, her thumb brushes the metal where the cheap enamel is chipped at the edge. Her laugh cracks open on a shaky breath.

"You kept this?" she whispers.

"You gave it to me."

"I snuck it in your pocket."

"Still counts."

Her mouth curves into that smile that wrecks me every time. "Okay," she says. "Spice it up, then." Her voice is all sugar and dare and I'm fucking gone for her.

Whatever thread of patience I was holding snaps.

Hauling her with me, I drop to the mattress and settle her into my lap, legs spread wide over mine.

She glances at the mirror, then tries to duck her head, but I catch her chin. With my thumb stroking her jaw, I force her eyes back up.

"No hiding, Firefly," I rasp against her ear. "You watch what happens when you say shit like that to me."

She lets out a quiet, helpless laugh. The kind that's half a dare, half surrender. But it dies in her throat when I fist the hem of her shirt and drag it up, slow, baring that soft skin inch by inch. She lifts her arms without me asking.

Good fucking girl.

Her shirt hits the floor. She's breathless, cheeks pink, eyes flicking from my mouth to the mirror and back again.

"You cold?" I murmur, my hands skimming her ribs, thumbing under the soft edge of her bra.

"No," she whispers, but her voice cracks when I mouth at her shoulder. "You're warm enough."

"Yeah," I growl, palming her breast, teasing her nipple until it peaks under my thumb. "I'm going to keep you warm. Going to keep you sore, too. You still aching from last night? From how many times I made you come on my cock?"

She shudders, hips rolling in my lap like she can't help it. Her breath catches when my hand drifts down, slipping under the waistband of those tight black leggings.

"Tell me," I rasp against her throat. "You sore from me?"

She nods, her breath a tiny broken thing when my fingers find how wet she already is. How ready. How perfect.

"It...it aches," she whispers, her hips bucking when I circle her clit, slow and teasing. "A good ache."

"That's mine," I growl, pressing a kiss under her ear as I work the leggings down her hips. She lifts, squirming to help me strip them off. But the fuzzy socks stay, because fuck, I like her that soft when I'm about to ruin her.

I palm myself through my jeans, rough, desperate. "You want me anyway?" I growl, dragging my cock out, the head flushed and leaking for her. "Want me to stretch you open again? Fuck that sore little cunt until you're dripping all over my lap?"

She whimpers when I line us up, back arched, her ass snug against my thighs.

"Yes," she pants, eyes locked on mine in the mirror. "Please, Liam—please—"

My tip nudges at her slick entrance, the mirror throwing her wide eyes and parted lips right back at me.

She turns her head, brushing her mouth over my jaw, so soft it almost breaks me.

"Fuck." I push in slow, dragging her hips down until she's seated all the way. Until she's full and the stretch is both brutal and perfect.

She moans, her knees trembling on either side of my thighs, the fuzzy socks brushing my jeans like some innocent halo around this filthy mess.

"Eyes up, Firefly," I pant, my palm flat on her belly, pressing just enough to feel myself inside her.

Her eyes flick to the mirror, catching the place where my cock disappears inside her, where she's spread wide and slick and fucking perfect.

A soft gasp escapes her, and it cracks something open in me. It splits me wide with how sweet she sounds, how she grips my forearm like she'll drown if I don't hold her steady.

I shift my grip, palm sliding up from her belly to her chest to cup her breast. My thumb teases over her nipple until it peaks under my touch. The sight of it in the mirror is fucking obscene—her back arched, her flushed tits in my hand while my cock disappears inside her over and over.

"Look at you," I growl, rolling her nipple between my fingers until she gasps, hips twitching helplessly. "So pretty like this. So fucking *mine*."

I drag her hips up slowly just to slam her back down again. The wet slap of it echoes soft and filthy in the warm quiet. "See how good you take me?"

She moans, her lashes fluttering as she locks on the mirror and sees my thick cock parting her. The slick mess of where we're joined.

"That ache you feel?" I murmur in her ear, voice frayed

at the edges. "That's mine. This pretty cunt is mine. All of you—fucking mine."

She whimpers, her nails biting into my thigh now where her hand has slipped back, clutching me like she needs something to anchor her to earth. Her other palm fists the edge of my knee, bracing herself as I rock her up and down my cock, slow and filthy, every slick slide of her making my balls tighten and my breath catch in my chest.

"Can feel you clench every time I touch you here," I rasp, tugging at her nipple just to hear her cry out. "You like that, Firefly? You like when I play with you like this?"

She nods frantically, her hips bucking when I roll my thumb lower, brushing her swollen clit while I thrust up into her. Her cry breaks into a soft, breathless moan when I pinch her nipple again, the shiver rippling through her so sweet I almost lose it.

"Fuck, look at us," I pant, mouth at her ear. "Look how you grip me—look at that messy little cunt, all stretched and dripping around me."

She moans louder, head falling back onto my shoulder, her legs trembling on either side of me. Her hand grips my thigh tighter, her breath coming in frantic little gasps that send heat curling low in my spine.

"You gonna come for me again, baby?" I rasp, voice raw at her ear as my fingers toy with her nipple and her clit all at once. "Gonna make a mess all over my cock while you watch yourself fall apart?"

"Liam—oh—" She breaks apart on my cock, her nails digging into my thigh while her whole body shudders so hard I swear I feel it in my chest. It's like she's got her hands wrapped around my fucking heart and she's squeezing it tight.

I can't hold off any longer. With her pussy still gripping me tight, my cock pulses, spilling deep inside her.

I hold her there, buried deep, my hand splayed wide over her belly, the other still cupping her breast like I can't bear to let go. My forehead drops to her shoulder, breath ragged, the air thick with heat and her soft, broken sounds.

"Jesus, Firefly," I rasp, pressing an open-mouthed kiss to her neck, tasting her sweat and that soft, clean smell of her. "You're gonna fucking kill me."

She huffs out a tired laugh, her fingers sliding from my thigh to my hair—tugging, petting, threading through it like she's piecing me back together strand by strand before placing a soft kiss to my stitched-up brow.

"Good," she whispers, voice wrecked but smug as hell. "Someone has to keep you humble, Hargrove."

I laugh against her skin, still high on the feeling of having her here.

She shifts in my lap, her slick heat squeezing me just right, and I hiss when she clenches, on purpose, that wicked glint in her eye when she catches my face in the mirror.

"You think you can just...keep me here?" she teases, breathless but sharp, her fingers tugging my hair back so she can make me meet her eyes. "Buy the place next door, sneak your way into my bed...my bookstore...my life?"

"Yeah," I smirk. "It worked, didn't it?"

She laughs. It's soft, sleepy, and so damn beautiful it hurts.

She shifts in my lap, her fingers tracing lazy circles on my chest, like she's trying to memorize every inch. We're a mess—warm and tangled up, the window glass still fogged behind us. I should get up and grab something to clean us up, but I can't help wanting to stay in this moment with her.

She tilts her head, searching my face. There's a question

in her eyes she doesn't quite say out loud, but I see it anyway. She's wondering if I'll really stay. If I want to. If she's enough to keep me here.

She doesn't know she's the only thing that could.

"Are you really sure about this?" she asks, voice low. "Staying here. Me."

I slide my hand up her thigh and squeeze. "Pretty sure the wine bar lease says I'm stuck with you."

She huffs a laugh against my jaw, pressing a quick kiss there. "Terrible business plan."

"Best plan I've ever had." I tip my head back, watching her like I can't believe she's mine to look at.

"You're not worried you'll get bored with small-town life?"

I raise a brow. "Small-town life, no. You?" I lean in closer, brushing my mouth against her cheek. "Never. I'll be too busy stealing all your romance books when you're not looking."

She laughs, warm and teasing. "You know I'll just steal them back."

Juniper's concern is expected. From her perspective, I'm changing my whole life to be here with her. What she doesn't realize is, my whole life changed the moment she kissed me. Since that moment, I've been working toward this life with her.

I brush my thumb over the curve of her hip, let myself look at her like maybe it'll help her see it from my side. She's it for me. "You know you're the only thing that makes any of this make sense, right?"

She bites her lip like she's trying not to smile too wide. "Well, when you say it like that...I guess it's fine if you stay."

I grin, tugging her closer until her laugh is muffled

against my mouth. "Good," I murmur. "Because I am not going anywhere."

# THIRTY

# JUNIPER

BY THE TIME we make it to my parents' house, it's snowing again. Soft, fat flakes that cling to the porch lights and turn the yard into a winter wonderland.

Inside, it's a riot of cinnamon and pine and too many people talking over each other. Stella's at the kitchen counter with my mom, trying to keep her from making a third pie *just in case*. Jasper is by the fireplace, arms crossed, watching Liam like he's debating whether to tackle him or hug him. Beck's already found the cookie tray and is stealth-eating sugar cookies behind the tree, thinking no one notices.

And Liam? He's at my side the whole time. His fingers brush mine when I pass him a mug of cider, his palm warm at the small of my back when Jasper corners him for a brotherly talk that I pretend not to overhear. Every time I look up, he's there. *Mine.*

It shouldn't feel this simple. But it does.

When my mom drags everyone into the living room for presents and polite chaos, Liam catches my wrist. His palm slides against mine, our fingers threading easy as breathing. He leans in, warm breath against my hair.

"Come here, Firefly." His voice is low, rough like he's been laughing too much today. Like he's not quite ready to share every part of this with everyone else just yet.

He tugs me down the hallway, past the old photos and the creaky floorboard we always tried to avoid when we were sneaking out at sixteen. We slip into my childhood bedroom where my aunt and uncle are staying. It's a little too pink, a little too small, and for a second, it's like time folds over on itself. Last year, it was this room and my heart in Liam's hands.

I turn to find him already close, so close. His eyes soft and a little sharp at the same time. It's a look that makes my knees wobble.

"I didn't say it earlier," he murmurs, voice so gentle my chest squeezes. "Not like this. Not the way I wanted to."

He cups my jaw, thumb brushing under my chin. His other hand slips around my waist, pulling me closer like he can't stand even an inch between us.

"I love you, Juniper," he says. Simple as that. Like it's the most obvious thing in the world. "I love you for every smart mouth thing you say, for every risk you take, for putting your heart out there and making me braver than I deserved to be. I love you. All of you. Always."

It hits me, soft but sharp, like the first breath after stepping inside from the cold. I feel it in every part of me.

"Say it back," he whispers, and he's smiling but his eyes are pleading. Like he's still the guy from last year, terrified and trying anyway.

I lift my hands to his face, brushing my thumbs over his obnoxiously perfect cheekbones, the scruff I love so much.

"I love you," I say, and it's so easy, so true I almost laugh.

"You and your possessive streak, and your over-the-top grand gestures. Your half-finished mugs of coffee all over the place and the way you argue with podcasts in the shower."

"So you've been listening to me in the shower?"

"It's hard not to."

His laugh breaks between us, then he kisses me like there's nothing left to prove. Like we have every Christmas morning after this one to get it right.

Somewhere downstairs, Beck yells that he's eating my share of pie if I don't come back. My mom's voice rises, trying to herd everyone through the chaos of gift unwrapping and dessert plates. The kids squeal about who got what. The whole house is alive with warmth and noise.

But none of it really registers because I'm here; in Liam's arms, warm and safe and exactly where I belong.

# EPILOGUE

## ONE MONTH LATER

## *JUNIPER*

The last customer leaves with a stack of romance paperbacks bundled in a pink ribbon, cheeks flushed from the cold. I watch through the frosted window as she disappears down Founders Street, the snow catching the glow from the twinkle lights overhead.

It's late, nearly closing, and while the bookstore still hums with its usual quiet warmth, I'm ready to leave it behind for the night. My coat's lying across the back counter, my lipstick freshly reapplied.

From the front windows I see the warm light spilling from behind the black-framed windows next door—Liam's wine bar, now alive with chatter and soft music. Both of us are woven into every inch of the place. The brass letters of *Juniper & Grove* glint under the streetlights dimmed by fresh falling January snow. It feels like the perfect start to the new year.

The past month has been a whirlwind. Snowy mornings spent sipping lattes and eating chocolate croissants, with no resolution to give them up. Quiet evenings reading while Liam poured over wine lists. And stolen kisses in the empty wine bar when no one was watching. Every moment has been building toward this night—the grand opening.

I take one last look around the bookstore—the dog-eared copy of *Pride & Prejudice* someone left in the free exchange bin, the stack of mugs still faintly scented with hot cocoa and cider—then grab my coat.

I'm buzzing with excitement, ready for the night ahead.

I step outside, the snow crunching softly underfoot. The glow from the sign warms the street. Juniper & Grove. Brass letters spelling out something bigger than either of us could have imagined.

Inside, the hum of voices, laughter, and clinking glasses wraps around me like a cozy blanket. I spot Stella chatting with her sister, Sadie, and her husband, Tom, near the bar, their smiles bright and easy. Jasper is close by, leaning casually against the wall with a warm smile on his face and a glass of red in his hand. Beck is by the wine racks, his laughter ringing out. Everyone has made a special trip back to Cedar Hollow for the occasion.

And Liam? He's behind the bar, sleeves rolled up, wearing that slow grin I could get lost in forever.

His eyes find mine, and he crosses the room without hesitation. His arms wrap around me, warm and steady.

"Hey," he says, voice low and familiar.

"Hey," I reply, hands pressed to his chest.

He pulls me close, just enough to feel the heat of him. "Ready for this?"

"For you? Always."

We share a quiet laugh and the bar's noise fades to background music.

He brushes a strand of hair behind my ear. "Good. Because I want you here with me, every step."

I lean into him, feeling like I've finally found my home.

"Everyone looks happy," I murmur, nodding toward the group.

Liam follows my gaze. "Yeah. It feels right. Like all the pieces finally fit."

I glance over at Jasper, whose easy smile lights up the room. Stella raises her glass in a subtle toast, and Cassie waves at me with that mischievous grin that always makes me laugh.

Beck pops up beside Liam, holding a plate of cookies. "Hey, don't forget the real party favors," he jokes, nudging Liam.

Liam chuckles and ruffles Beck's hair. "Thanks, man. We couldn't have done this without you."

I lean my head against Liam's shoulder, watching the people I love gathered here. My family, my friends, and the man who's become my home.

Together, we step further into the night—into this life, this place, this story we're writing side by side.

# THANK YOU

Dear Reader,

Thank you for taking the time to read my book. I hope you enjoyed Juniper and Liam! There are so many books to choose from, so thank you for spending your precious time reading mine. If you have a minute, please consider leaving a review for Booked for the Holidays. Reviews help indie authors so much!

XO, Erin

# ACKNOWLEDGMENTS

Thank you to my family, Eric and my children, for always supporting me in this career that is a roller coaster of emotions (so many emotions!)

Thank you to Shayna for helping me create this fun and festive cover! I appreciate your creativity, your friendship, and our coffee walks.

Thank you to my copy editor, Chelly, it's always a pleasure working with you. And, thank you to Emma for proofreading...I loved reading your comments!

# ABOUT THE AUTHOR

Erin Hawkins is a spicy romcom author who lives in Colorado with her husband, three children, and mini Bernedoodle, Scout. She enjoys reading, working out, spending time in the mountains with her family, reality TV, and brunch that lasts all day.